PRESIDENTIAL SHIFT

BOOK 4 OF THE CORPS JUSTICE SERIES

BY

C. G. COOPER

PRESIDENTIAL SHIFT

Book 4 of the *Corps Justice* Series

Warning: *This story is intended for mature audiences and contains profanity and violence.*

Dedications

To our amazing troops serving all over the world,
thank you for your bravery and service.

Semper Fidelis

Chapter 1
Vienna, Virginia
7:04am, December 15th

THE RUNNER SPED past a woman pushing a lime green jogging stroller. Despite his fast pace, the jogger didn't look winded. Adjusting his white Adidas cap as he turned into the public park, he scanned the area from behind Oakley running glasses. His brown hair could barely be seen peeking out.

There was a hidden alcove of trees off to the right and he ran that way. Headed toward a row of park benches, he waved to a thin man seated wearing a heavy parka. The dark-complexioned man looked up from an Arabic newspaper at the sound of the man's footfalls and returned the wave with a smile.

The runner floated to a halt in front of the bench surrounded by a tight copse of pine.

"Morning, Mansoor!" the runner offered with a smile.

"And a good morning to you, Richard," the Middle Easterner replied, in slightly accented English. "Are you finished with your exercise already?"

The man nodded. "Yeah, just a quick run today. Probably head to the gym after work. Mind if I stretch while we chat?"

"Not at all. May I offer you some of my tea?" Mansoor asked.

"Is it the stuff your cook makes?"

"It is."

"That stuff is amazing. Much better than the crap you get at Starbucks."

Mansoor nodded. "It is one of the many things I miss about my country."

While the young runner Mansoor knew as Richard stretched, the Arab poured out a cup of tea. Richard glanced up casually to see his friend pouring a second cup, and without taking his eyes off Mansoor, he reached down and looked to be adjusting the sock around his ankle.

"Funny I keep bumping into you like this," Richard said.

Mansoor looked up from his tea. "If I was a suspicious man, I would think you might be following me, Richard," he responded playfully.

His companion shrugged. "What can I say? I guess I'm into good-looking Arabs with hot tea."

Blood rose to Mansoor's face as he waved away the compliment. They'd only met days earlier, but had quickly found they believed in many of the same things. Most importantly, they'd spoken at length about the wars still being waged in the Middle East. Mansoor had found it comforting to meet such an enlightened, and handsome, American. It hadn't taken long to figure out that Richard was probably gay, although his last comment was the most overt flirting either one had yet attempted.

"Why don't you come have your tea?"

Richard nodded and sat down next to his friend. He took the paper cup and held it up in a toast. "To new friends."

The two men tapped their cups together and took sips of their tea. Mansoor savored the taste of his past. A few minor errands, and soon he would return to his country. He smiled at the thought.

Richard looked up from his tea and cocked his head. "What are you thinking about?"

Mansoor shook away his thoughts and focused on his prize. "I was thinking that maybe we should do dinner sometime. What do you think?"

Richard's light complexion flushed slightly as he took another sip of his tea.

"What is it, my friend?" asked Mansoor, stroking his slick goatee carefully.

Richard shook his head as if to say he was too embarrassed to respond

"Come, Richard. You know you can tell me anything. What is the matter?"

"I don't know if I should tell you. It's...it's kind of a secret."

Richard took another hurried sip of his tea. Mansoor placed a hand on his friend's shoulder.

"Please tell me," he whispered. His oversized obsidian eyes glinted with excitement.

Richard nodded and leaned in to whisper in his ear. Mansoor shuddered involuntarily and moved in closer. Richard used his left hand to bring Mansoor's head near. It was an almost intimate gesture. His lips were right next to Mansoor's ear.

Richard whispered, "I have to kill you now."

Mansoor's eyes widened as the killer inserted a double-edged blade into his throat. He struggled against the pull, but the executioner held on to his head and twisted the knife, forcing the man's lifeblood out in a steady flow. The assassin was careful to cant his victim's head to avoid the gushing blood.

The Middle Easterner's eyes glazed and his movement stopped. Moving quickly, the assassin laid the dead man down on the bench and covered him with the open newspaper, avoiding the pooling blood. Next he wiped his blade on the man's jacket and returned it to its sheath.

He heard a rustling from the woods and turned to see another man dressed in running gear walking toward him.

"You okay?" asked Daniel Briggs, the blonde pony-tailed former Marine sniper.

"I'm good," Cal Stokes answered. He looked down at his watch and exhaled. "Let's head back to the hotel and get cleaned up. We've gotta be at the Oval office in two hours."

Chapter 2
The White House, Washington, D.C.
10:15am, December 15th

THEY'D BEEN WAITING for the president for fifteen minutes.

"You think we should call him on the fifteen-minute rule?" asked Cal with a smirk.

Daniel returned the look.

"I'm not sure that would go over well."

"You're probably right. Our professors at U.Va didn't like it much when we up and left after waiting for them for fifteen minutes."

"Is that really a rule?"

"Of course. That's why they call…"

Before Cal could finish his sentence, the president stepped into the Oval Office followed by two aides.

"Cal, Daniel, I'm really sorry I'm late."

Both Marines stood to shake the president's hand.

"Doesn't bother me, Mr. President. It was Daniel that was about to enact the fifteen minute rule," said Cal with a straight face.

Daniel glared at his friend. There was an awkward pause as the president glanced between the two men. A small grin found its way to Cal's face and the president chuckled.

"You Marines never let up, do you?"

"No, sir," answered Cal. "Keeps us on our toes."

The two men standing with binders behind the president stared in shock. Cal winked at them.

The president laughed again.

"Don't mind Mr. Stokes, fellas. We go way back. Would you excuse us?"

One of the aides, a freckled-faced redhead, looked like he was going to say something. He changed his mind and the two men departed.

The President jotted something down on a notepad.

"Can I get you two anything? Coffee, water?" he asked.

"No, sir," the Marines answered in unison.

"Give me one minute and then we'll head down to the situation room."

Cal looked at Daniel with one eyebrow raised. The sniper shrugged his shoulders in response.

A minute later, the president ripped off the sheet of paper, folded it, and stuck it in his pants pocket.

"Let's go."

They followed him out of the Oval Office and through the White House maze. Secret Service agents shadowed them quietly. Few people they passed even looked up from their work. To them, seeing the president was nothing new.

After being cleared, the trio stepped into the secure conference room. There was one man waiting for them.

"What are you doing here, Brandon?" Cal said.

Newly elected Senator Brandon Zimmer, a Democrat from Massachusetts, rose to greet his friends. They shook hands.

"It was a last minute thing. The president called me yesterday and said he'd been trying to get you to come in for a couple months." He scanned Cal's placid face. They'd become close over the previous months, with Zimmer often calling on Cal to play devil's advocate. "What have you been up to?"

"Nothing special. Just a little busy."

Brandon looked at his friend for a second longer, waiting for further explanation.

"Why don't we all have a seat, gentlemen," the president suggested.

The four men took seats at one end of the long conference table.

"First, I'd like to once again thank you for saving my tail before the election. I will never forget it."

Cal, Daniel and even Brandon had been part of a dicey operation months earlier to uncover a plot by Japanese imperialists and Brandon's own father, Senator Richard Zimmer, to kill the president and take over the country. Richard Zimmer was now dead. It was a bullet from Brandon's own hand that had done the deed.

The event cemented the relationship between Cal and Brandon. It had also tied them to the president. They'd all agreed that the assassination attempt would be kept secret. So far it had, and the president had won re-election without the sympathy votes that such a revelation would have stirred.

"Second, I know I don't have to tell you this, but what I'm about to say stays in this room."

The others nodded.

The president took a weary breath. His face sagged a bit as he looked down. When he lifted his head, his eyes looked tired.

"I have reason to believe that someone within my administration is leaking information."

His small audience waited for him to explain.

"I know what you're probably thinking. Leaks are as common as liars on Capitol Hill. But...this feels different."

He paused as if searching for the right words. None came. The anguish on his face was plain.

Cal broke the silence.

"Maybe if you start from the beginning, Mr. President?"

The president nodded and began.

"After the attack in Las Vegas, everything seemed to go back to normal. Other than the usual threats, nothing new came up. Right around the election, I'm not sure exactly what day, I kept seeing the same man in the crowds. He wasn't part of any of my details. The man didn't do anything except act like any other onlooker. I can't really explain what I saw. It was more about what I felt. It was like he was watching me. I asked the Secret Service about him, but by that time he had disappeared.

"Election night rolls around and it's all excitement. We were leading in the polls and, of course, eventually won. That's when things changed."

"How, sir?" asked Cal.

The president looked up from his brooding with a half smile.

"Sorry. I must be tired." He took a moment to gather his thoughts. "I won't sit here and pretend that politics is a clean sport. You know as well as I do that there are a lot of shady characters running around D.C. trying to grab all the power they can. I knew that going in. Before my first term, I made some subtle promises. A wealthy donor would give X amount of money to my campaign, and I promised to consider his help in the future. Senator Zimmer can tell you that it's as common as church on Sunday."

Brandon nodded.

"After the attempt on my life that you gentlemen so bravely thwarted, I...I started thinking about my legacy. I started..."

He glanced over to see that Cal's face had hardened.

"Did I say something wrong, Cal?" asked the president.

"It's none of my business, Mr. President."

"What's none of your business?"

"How you run the country."

"I wouldn't have asked you here if that were the case."

"I'm sorry?"

"Why don't you say what you were thinking? I'd rather know it up front before going further."

Daniel cleared his throat and caught Cal's eye. The sniper shook his head. Cal ignored the warning.

"I don't like politics, Mr. President. Senator Zimmer can tell you that. I couldn't care less about the back room deals you make to get in office. To me it's a bunch of horse shit. You make a bunch of promises and then turn the other way."

"Is that the reason you didn't come see me the day I called?"

There was no accusation in the president's tone. Just a question.

"That was part of it. The other part, that you might not know, is that I'd just buried one of my best friends. Put the two together and yeah, you could say I wasn't exactly in the mood to visit."

"I'm sorry for your loss," offered the president. "I didn't know."

"Thank you."

"Would you like to go on?"

Cal rubbed his eyes slowly.

"It's not that I don't think you're a nice guy, Mr. President. I came because I'm a Marine and I respect the office that you hold. I don't agree with your policies. In fact, I think they've weakened our country. Your push for social welfare reform is giving people a free pass. Americans' sense of entitlement is obscene. Whatever happened to an honest day's work and helping your neighbor? Now it's all about how the government can support me. Me, me, me."

The president nodded grimly.

"I understand how you feel," the president said.

"I'm not so sure about that, Mr. President."

"I think you'd be surprised." He stopped and smiled. "Your reservations actually play perfectly into why I called you."

Cal's face scrunched in confusion.

"How is that?"

"Let me back up a bit. I'm not a stupid man, Cal. I may have walked into the presidency a little naïve, but I've kept my eyes and ears open. I understand that many of the initiatives I first sought to introduce were well meaning, but...misguided. What I failed to see was man's greed. I've watched as billions of dollars have been wasted on junk programs. I've seen my constituency beg for milk money and spend it on drugs. I've shaken hands with members of Congress only to see them take their money and funnel it into their pet projects. Most Americans have no idea the level of corruption that exists within their own country. I can tell you that I'm quietly trying to root out these elements."

"So why do you need us?"

The president looked at each of his three visitors.

"Someone is trying to stop me."

"Stop you from doing what?"

"From cleaning up Washington."

There was only silence in the conference room. An amused look fell across Cal's face.

"No offense, Mr. President, but that sounds a bit grandiose."

The president chuckled.

"I know how it sounds, but I'm dead serious."

This time it was Brandon who broke the uncomfortable silence.

"And how do you propose to do that, Mr. President?"

"I don't know yet. I've been putting out feelers to some of my most trusted advisers. They're all telling me it can't be done. One of them even had the nerve to tell me to let it lie."

The president shook his head angrily.

"I will not stand by and watch this country be ripped apart. We have enough enemies overseas. Killing ourselves from within is suicide."

"How can we help, Mr. President?" asked Cal. His demeanor had calmed. He could see the president had changed. Now it was time to see how much.

"I need two things. First, help me come up with a way to dig out these parasites and expose them for what they are. Second, find out who is trying to sabotage my efforts."

Cal exhaled.

"I'm not sure you want me doing that, sir."

"Why not?"

"I don't think you'd approve of my methods."

"And if I did?"

"Then I don't think you'd like what we'd find."

The President put his chin in his palm.

"You mean you think this will lead back to me."

"Shit rolls downhill, Mr. President."

Instead of being angry, the president laughed.

"Did you learn that in the Marine Corps, Staff Sergeant?"

"I did, sir."

"So tell me, what happens in the Marine Corps when a unit is found to be ineffective or negligent?"

"They go after the commanding officer. But that doesn't happen in Washington."

"I beg your pardon?"

"Unless a politician murders someone or sneaks gold bricks out of Fort Knox, they won't be fired. Let me equate it to the civilian world. If a CEO leads his corporation into bankruptcy or even has bad quarterly earnings, the board lets the CEO go. That doesn't happen here. It's okay for politicians to play with our money, waste it, misspend it, and yet they keep getting reelected."

"And you don't put any blame on the American people?" asked the president, eyebrow raised.

"Of course I do, sir, but it starts at the top. If I were a CEO and led my company poorly, I would feel it was my obligation, no, my duty, to step down."

"You know I can't do that, Cal."

"You asked, Mr. President," Cal answered with a shrug.

"So what do you propose we do when we find these corrupt officials?"

Cal grinned. "Go after them with everything we've got."

"And how would we do that?"

"We'd run it case by case. We've been known to get creative."

"You'd have to promise me that no one would get hurt."

"You mean physically?"

The president nodded.

"That wasn't my plan anyway, sir. There are plenty of ways to skin a cat."

"So you're saying you'll do it?"

Cal looked to his two friends.

"I'll do it on two conditions."

The president's eyes narrowed.

"And what would those conditions be?"

"One, I bring in anyone I need."

"And the second?"

"The gloves are off, Mr. President. We expose these crooks to the world. No second chances."

"Agreed," replied the president without hesitation.

"So, where would you like—." Cal was cut off when five Secret Service agents burst into the room.

"What is it?" asked the president, more annoyed than concerned.

The first agent into the room answered. "There's been an attack, Mr. President. We need to get you to safety."

"Where?"

"At the Air and Space Museum."

The president's eyes widened. Cal, Daniel and Brandon looked confused.

"The first lady?"

"She was wounded by the blast and taken to the closest hospital for emergency surgery."

The president stood up from his chair and moved toward his security detail. He looked to his guests.

"I'm sorry, gentlemen, but if you'll excuse me."

The three men rose quickly and moved in the direction of the exit. One of the large agents put his hand to stop them from coming closer. Cal looked annoyed.

"Mr. President," said the lead agent.

The president turned to face him.

"There's more, sir."

"What do you mean?"

The agent's stoic face hesitated momentarily.

"The vice president is dead."

Chapter 3
Smithsonian Institution National Air & Space Museum, Washington, D.C.
11:09am, December 15th

AT THE DIRECTION of the president, Cal and Daniel accompanied one of the Secret Service vehicles heading to the scene of the deadly attack. The agents hadn't been happy about it, but took their orders.

They sat in the back of the armored SUV as it maneuvered through the winding streets of D.C. Tourists stared as processions of siren-wailing vehicles sped in the same direction.

"How many people were hurt?" Cal asked the agent sitting in the front passenger seat.

The man held up an index finger as he listened to the chatter on his earpiece. Cal waited. Finally the man turned.

"Initial estimates say forty-two civilians killed, another fifty wounded. We lost four agents along with the vice president."

"I'm sorry," offered Cal.

The man nodded.

"You want to tell me why the president asked for you two to come along?"

Cal shrugged. "I'm in the dark, just like you."

The agent stared at his unwanted passengers, and then huffed.

"Just do me a favor and stay out of the way, okay?"

"No problem."

The agent glanced at the driver and turned back to listening to his earpiece.

Daniel nudged Cal and whispered, "What do you want me to do?"

"Let's just go see what we can see. Who knows, maybe two dumb Marines will be able to do some good in a shitty situation.

✚ ✚ ✚

They arrived at the scene minutes later. The attack had occurred on the National Mall side of the museum, so their vehicle parked along the grass edge of Jefferson Drive SW. A mix of metro police and FBI had cordoned off two full blocks. Everyone looked on edge, weapons drawn.

Cal and Daniel got out of the vehicle and looked up at the devastation. Half of the windowed entrance of the Air and Space Museum was gone. Glass littered the ground both inside and out.

The driver handed each a badge on a lanyard.

"Put these on," the man ordered. "Remember what I said. You can take a look around, but stay out of the way."

The two Marines nodded and were left alone. They surveyed the scene.

"How do you think they did it?" Cal asked his companion.

"I'd say it was some kind of mortar or rocket."

"That's what I was thinking. Let's go take a look inside."

Federal personnel rushed around them as they ascended the stairs. It looked like the majority of the wounded had already been triaged and the worst of the injured had been transported to local hospitals. Near the welcome desk was a growing row of bodies laid side by side. They looked to be covered with curtains that someone had ripped down from inside the building.

Museum pieces that were once hanging now sat on the ground or dipped precariously. Everyone avoided walking under them, and workers were already trying to secure them in place.

Cal pointed over to where the center of the carnage appeared to be. They had to dodge pools of blood as they walked carefully around debris. A crew of forensic men and women were taking pictures, using large cameras with high wattage flashes.

Cal tapped one of the photographers on the shoulder. The man turned and looked down at Cal's badge. He adjusted his thick glasses as he sized up the stranger.

"Can I help you?"

"Is this where the vice president was standing?"

"Yeah. There was a podium right there," he pointed to a spot on ground now gouged and twisted. "Witnesses say he was introducing the first lady when the explosion happened."

"Where was the first lady standing?"

"Over there, behind that corner, waiting to be announced."

Cal and Daniel looked to where he was pointing. Black streaks marred the wall's sturdy white surface.

"Hey, I need to get back to taking these pictures."

Cal let the man get back to his work.

"Let's see where the first lady was standing," Cal suggested.

Walking around the corner, they found a small area marked with orange cones. In the center of the cones was an index card taped to ground. It was labeled, *First Lady*. Blood spatter streaked angrily along the floor.

"That's a lot of blood," Cal thought aloud.

"Yeah. She was darned close to the explosion," said Daniel.

They took another loop through the site, and then exited the way they'd come. Federal agents and emergency personnel continued to stream in and out of the entrance as the Marines walked out onto Jefferson Drive. Daniel cupped his hands over his eyes and surveyed the area.

"What are you thinking?" Cal asked.

Daniel pointed across the lawn. "What's that building over there?"

Cal squinted. "I think that's the National Gallery of Art."

"Let's go take a look."

Cal and Daniel scanned the vicinity as they walked across the now crowded National Mall.

"There don't seem to be many vantage points on this side of the museum," said Cal.

"I was thinking the same thing. They would've needed some serious weaponry to shoot from across the lawn. From looking at that point of impact, it reminded me of some of those laser guided systems we used in Afghanistan."

"Those things are pretty big. How the hell did they get it in here without being seen?"

Daniel didn't answer and continued to inspect the scene.

As they neared the opposite side of the Mall, Cal pointed.

"Looks like they've already got the area cordoned off."

Masked men in black SWAT suits guarded the entrance to the columned structure. Cal and Daniel showed their badges and were ushered through.

Cal walked toward an agent barking orders.

"Excuse me."

The agent turned, an annoyed look already plastered on his face. He glanced down at Cal's badge.

"Can I help you?"

"Find anything?" asked Cal.

"I don't mean to be rude, but can't you see that we're pretty busy around here?"

"We're not here to get in the way. The president sent us over to take a look around. That's all we're doing."

The annoyed agent stared at both men for a moment as if deciding whether to continue the conversation.

"And what makes you so special?"

Cal shrugged. "We're not. Just a couple of dumb grunts."

The agent actually grinned.

"Okay, dumb grunt. We're trying to find out where the weapon was launched from."

"Going with line of sight first?" Daniel questioned.

"Yeah. The most obvious place was here because of the clear shot."

"Any surveillance video?"

"Not yet. Some of our guys are working on that now."

"Have you found pieces of the warhead?"

"Just fragments so far. Forensics is still putting it together."

"What's your gut telling you?" Cal interrupted.

The agent shook his head. "I'm not sure yet. One thing I will say is that shot was a little too precise."

Cal nodded. "That's what we were just talking about. Would've been one helluva shot unless they used some kind of laser-guided system."

A policeman interrupted their conversation.

"We've got the video you wanted."

The agent thanked the cop.

"You two want to come see?"

"If you don't think we'll be in the way, sure," answered Cal.

They followed the police officer and the Secret Service agent back down the stairs and into the sunlight. There was an emergency response vehicle laden with antennas parked at the base of the steps. The back door of the large vehicle was open and the four men piled in.

Technicians manned the impressive array of computers lining the sides of the mobile command post. The officer pointed to a tech near the front of the space.

"He'll show you."

The Secret Service agent walked up to the man.

"What have you got?"

Without looking up from his work, the tech answered. "I've got views from three different angles. It's not much."

"What do you mean?"

"From my initial analysis, there's no obvious perpetrator."

"What about the explosive? Any sign of where it came from?"

"That's what's really weird. I thought there'd be some kind of back blast or rooster tail, but there isn't."

"But whatever it was did come from outside the building, correct?"

"Yes. It's just a blur, but it definitely came from outside. Here, let me show you."

There was silence as the visitors watched the scene unfold. One second the entrance was there and the next there was an explosion. The angle of the camera should have given a perfect vantage point for any incoming rounds.

"Can you clear up that image?" asked the agent.

"This is the best I can do for now. Once I get back to the lab, I'll be able to scrub it."

"What about you guys? Any thoughts?"

Cal and Daniel stared at the monitor. A look of recognition lit Daniel's eyes.

"What is it?" Cal asked.

Daniel reached over the tech's shoulder and grabbed the mouse. He slowly moved the video forward and back.

"I've seen that type of impact before," he said.

"Where?" demanded the agent.

"Overseas."

Chapter 4
Washington, D.C.
12:20pm, December 15th

DANIEL EXPLAINED. "It's what I thought, Cal. That looks exactly like a laser-guided bomb dropped from the air. But, any explosives I've seen would've destroyed half the building."

"Are you saying you think this was a military-grade weapon?" the Secret Service agent asked.

"Something quite a bit smaller, but yes. I think you need to find out what was flying overhead when the attack happened. You'll also want to see if you can pinpoint whoever was painting the target with the laser. I guess they could've used a homing device, but wouldn't your sweep of the museum have caught that?" said Daniel.

The agent nodded. "Something that accurate would've been planted on the vice president or in the podium. Both were clean." He looked down at his vibrating phone. "I've gotta run. Thanks for your help."

The big agent quickly made his way out of the vehicle, already on his phone.

"You guys need to see anything else?" asked the tech.

"No thanks," Cal said. "We'll get out of your hair."

They thanked the man and made their way out and onto the crowded street. Cal walked back toward the Air and Space Museum.

"I don't like the smell of this," Cal muttered.

"Me neither. This airspace is supposed to be sealed. I'd love to know how someone broke through."

Cal shrugged. "Not really our problem right now. I'm sure the Secret Service will figure it out. Let's head back to the White House and get our car."

They walked to a side street and hailed a cab.

+ + +

The man in the Redskins ball cap stood in the middle of the crowd, watching. He'd nonchalantly taped the events with his small video camera. No one gave him a second glance. He looked just like the rest of the tourists pushing to get a better shot of the wreckage.

With a bored look on his face, he moved away from the crowd and walked north. He palmed a small device he'd detached from the side of his camcorder. Blowing his nose loudly into a Kleenex, he discreetly wrapped the gadget in the used tissue and threw it into one of the many trashcans lining the mall.

There was a small hybrid car waiting at the corner to pick him up. He looked back one last time as he got in, and then left the scene.

✛ ✛ ✛

Cal and Daniel got back to the White House after a tough slog through the packed streets. It looked like every agency in the U.S. government was sending teams to the Air and Space Museum. They'd even seen four Marine light armored vehicles (LAVs) rolling the way they'd come.

When they got to their car, it was completely blocked in.

"Dammit," Cal grumbled.

"Let's go find out how we can get it out of there," Daniel suggested.

The White House entrance was a complete zoo. Staffers were running around yelling to colleagues, cell phones plastered to their ears. Security had quadrupled. Luckily, they still had the passes the Secret Service agent had given them. After triple checking their identification and receiving an extra thorough pat down, they were allowed back into the White House.

They made their way toward the Oval Office. Walking their way was Senator Zimmer. He was speaking to an aide as he hurried.

"Senator," said Cal.

Sen. Zimmer looked up.

"Give me a minute, Ted," he said to his assistant. "What going on, guys? Find anything at Air and Space?"

"Not really," answered Cal. "Is there somewhere we can talk?"

Zimmer nodded and led them to a tiny office that looked more like a closet.

"Somebody works in here?" asked Cal.

Zimmer smirked. "The perks of working in a building designed hundreds of years ago. So what did you find?"

Cal briefed the senator on little they knew.

"Do you really think someone snuck a missile into D.C. airspace?"

Daniel answered. "Probably not a missile. That would've flashed on radar. Besides, I've heard they have hidden surface to air batteries all over the city. We think it was probably some kind of smart bomb."

"Are you sure?"

"About eighty percent, sir," said Daniel.

"That's not good. Not good at all," said Zimmer.

"How's the first lady doing?" Cal asked.

"I just got word from the president. They haven't released this to the media yet, so keep it quiet. She had a good bit of shrapnel in her legs, and lost a lot of blood.

Luckily, they got her to the hospital pretty fast and were able to get her stable. She's sedated, but the doctor seems to think she'll make a full recovery."

"Well that's good. How about the president?"

"Between you and me, he's kind of in shock, I think. It's one thing to lose a bunch of Americans. Add to that the death of your vice president and the injuries to his wife..."

Cal and Daniel nodded.

"So what's the plan? Does he still want us doing what we talked about earlier?" asked Cal.

"Let's assume that he does. The attack doesn't really change anything. What do you need from me?"

Cal stared at the ground for a beat. "I want to make sure we're all on the same page. You know how we operate, Brandon. When I find out who's been playing around with government money, we're on full assault. Nobody is safe. I'm not sure the president gets that."

"I think he does, Cal. You heard what he said. Remember how I used to be before our trip to Vegas?"

Cal knew what the senator meant. Zimmer had been a self-absorbed and naïve politico before being blackmailed by a secret group of Japanese imperialists. He'd experienced a rude awakening in the aftermath.

"What if this comes back to him? Worse, what if it comes back to you?" asked Cal.

"I think I'm too new to have many skeletons. Besides, you guys know the worst of it. As for the president, that's his call. If the trail leads back to him, I think he'll own up to it."

Zimmer noticed the glower on his friend's face.

"If he tries to back out of it, I'll stand with you, Cal. I promise."

The two men stared at each other. Finally, Cal rolled his eyes and exhaled.

"I'll assume that's a yes?" asked Brandon.

"As long as you're the glue that binds us to the president."

They all shook hands and spent five more minutes outlining their plan.

+ + +

The man in the Redskins cap cowered in the corner of the dingy crack house.

"I did just what you told me to do!" he pleaded. "It's not my fault she made it."

Two men stood over him. One held a large caliber revolver pointed straight at the unfortunate underling.

"You and your partner said this should've been easy. Don't worry, we'll be talking to your buddy soon enough. He's on his way here now."

"But...but he won't be able to tell you anything different. That warhead was made to your exact specifications. It should have killed everyone in the gallery."

"Well it didn't and now I have to tell my boss that someone fucked up. You think I should tell him that *I* fucked up? I don't think so."

Without warning, he nudged his companion. His associate depressed the trigger and the bullet exited just underneath the Redskins cap a split second later.

"You want me to put him somewhere?" the man with the gun asked.

"Just leave him there."

The sound of a car pulling into the dirt drive crept into the house.

"Let's go take care of the other guy."

Chapter 5
Washington, D.C.
3:49pm, December 15th

BEFORE THEY COULD leave the White House, an intern found them. The president wanted to see them before they left town.

"I have a car waiting for you, gentlemen. It will take you over to the hospital."

Cal looked at Daniel resignedly.

"Lead on," said Cal.

They were both surprised to see a four vehicle motorcade waiting for them.

"I thought you said a car was waiting for us."

"This'll get you through the traffic," said the intern, who then turned and headed back into the White House.

✚ ✚ ✚

They arrived at MedStar Washington Hospital Center soon after. The Marines followed their new security detail through the various checkpoints manned by Secret Service and Marine sentries.

"You ever seen anything like this?" Cal muttered to Daniel.

"No way."

There were no less than thirty security personnel on the floor holding the first lady. The president was alone with his wife as they walked in. He looked up from the conversation.

"Cal, Daniel, you haven't met the first lady, have you?" His eyes were just barely tinged with red. Minus the loosened tie, he still looked the power part.

"No, sir," answered Cal. "Pleasure to meet you, ma'am."

"Are these the gentlemen you have helping you with your little project, honey?" The first lady's face looked drawn, and yet her eyes still burned with confidence.

The president nodded. "I figured unleashing a couple Marines might do some much needed feather-ruffling."

"Thank you for coming," she told Cal and Daniel. "Now if you'll please excuse me, I think I need to take a little nap."

"I'll be out in a minute, guys," said the president.

Cal and Daniel stepped out of room and waited patiently for the Commander in Chief to emerge. It didn't take more than a minute before he stepped out.

Motioning to the two friends, he guided them to another patient room that was empty. Daniel closed the door behind them.

"What did you find?" The president asked.

Cal relayed the same information they'd given Senator Zimmer. The president grimaced.

"You really think it's possible for someone to sneak a warhead into the most controlled airspace we have?"

"That's what we think, sir," replied Cal. "I'm sure the Secret Service is keeping you in the loop. They'll know for certain soon."

Nodding, the president paced the length of the room.

"This doesn't change what we talked about this morning, gentlemen. I was dead serious about exposing the crooks in this town."

"I understand, Mr. President. I've got our people digging as we speak. Have you thought about how you're going to handle the politicians we uncover?"

"I promised you that I'm all-in. Once they're exposed, the law will do the rest."

"Fair enough."

"Is there anything you need from me?" asked the president.

"I think we've got everything we need. One last thing, sir. I don't think we should be seen with you from here on out. You're already taking a chance of having this land in your lap. I don't want to give the enemy any more ammunition."

"How will I know if your investigation is progressing?"

Cal smirked. "Just keep checking the news, sir."

✚ ✚ ✚

Two men left the dilapidated tenement through the back door. As if on cue, a muffled boom sounded and a fire quickly engulfed the house. The multiple incendiary devices they'd installed were doing their job well. It would take the authorities a while to identify the bodies inside. That was if they even took the time to do DNA testing on the deceased. What was two more dead bodies in a crack house?

Chapter 6
SSI Headquarters II, Camp Cavalier, Charlottesville, VA
6:32am, December 16th

CAL AND DANIEL had driven back to Charlottesville the night before. They could've flown in one of SSI's private jets, but Cal wanted the time in the car to think.

They woke early and headed to Neil Patel's office to see what kind of progress the computer genius had made.

The Marines found their friend scrolling and clicking through gibberish-looking computer screens. Neil looked up from his work as they entered.

"I was wondering when you two would be visiting me. Did you bring any coffee?"

Cal held up a large to-go coffee mug he'd grabbed from the compound's mess hall.

"Three creams and four sugars. I don't know how you drink that, Neil."

"What can I say? I like it sweet."

Neil shifted around in his chair to grab the coffee.

"How's the leg doing?" asked Daniel, pointing down to Neil's prosthetic limb.

"Better now. I think this last adjustment did it." Neil sipped his coffee and swiveled back to his terminals. "I've got something for you, Cal."

Cal looked over his friends shoulder eagerly. "What did you find?"

Neil laughed. "This was almost too easy. Hacking into politicians' email accounts was a snap. I've got some juicy stuff and I'll probably have audio and video soon too."

"How the hell are you getting audio and video?"

"A couple ways. You'd be surprised how many of these people record their conversations. They're probably thinking about using them as insurance in case things go south with their contacts. Unfortunately for them, if they're accessed, we can use it against them. The way I'm getting video is through public and private security cameras. My facial recognition software does all the heavy lifting. It's already picked up some good clips. The hard part will be sifting through all the incoming data. Any thoughts on how you want me to prioritize?"

"Let's start with the top down," Cal suggested. "Maybe we'll be able to kill two birds with one stone. Target the president's top advisers and aides first. I'm sure that'll branch off soon enough."

Neil entered a few lines of code, and then looked up again. "I should have a couple dossiers soon."

+ + +

Their next stop was to see Cal's cousin and CEO of SSI Travis Haden. Cal knocked once and entered Travis's office. The former SEAL was on the phone with his bare feet propped up on the desk. He wore a sweat-drenched olive drab t-shirt that accentuated his bulging muscles. Travis motioned for the two Marines to have a seat.

"That's right. I'll pick you up at seven." Travis hung up the phone and swung his feet off the desk.

"Another one of your girlfriends, Trav?" Cal asked.

His cousin ignored the comment, used to the ribbing. "How was your trip?"

Cal ran through the highlights of the previous day's excursion.

"I assume Neil's already digging?" asked Travis once the recitation ended.

"He is. We're meeting for lunch to go over what he's got so far."

"What can I do to help?"

"The same as usual. Give me anything I want." Cal grinned.

Travis didn't reciprocate the look. Instead, he looked over at the sniper everyone called Snake Eyes.

"Daniel, can you give us a minute?"

Daniel started to get up out of his seat.

"Oh great! I'm in trouble now. Cousin Travis is gonna give me a scolding. Stay here, Daniel. I think I know where this is going."

Daniel looked between the two men. Technically they were both his bosses. In any other place Daniel might have left, but at SSI things were different. Here, Daniel was an equal and highly valued part of the team. When he spoke, people listened. Besides, he'd pledged himself to Cal months before. Daniel sat back down in his chair. Travis shrugged.

"Fine. It's probably better that you stay anyway." Travis opened a drawer and pulled out a blue folder a half inch thick. He laid it on the desk. "I need to talk to you about the last couple months. Now, I'm not saying..."

Cal huffed and said, "Just spit it out. I'm a big boy, remember?"

"Okay. Some of us are a little concerned about the number of operations you've been on recently."

"Who's we?"

"Me, Dunn and Marge."

"Not Doc Higgins?" Dr. Higgins was SSI's resident psychologist and expert interrogator. If you wanted to delve into a man's mind or carve out information, there were none better that Higgins.

"Not Higgins."

"Huh. That's funny. I would've thought that if someone was worried about me killing a bunch of bad guys it would be our shrink."

"I can't say I'm not surprised, but when I asked Doc about it, he told me that you know your limits."

"I do."

"So am I allowed to ask you about your targets?"

"I CC you on everything I greenlight."

"How about this guy you took out yesterday? Mans..."

"Mansoor Abbas, also went by Mansoor Daher, Manny Halabi and a few other names. Friend of Hezbollah, al Qaeda and some other upstart terrorist organizations. Had ties to terrorist funding coming from Saudi Arabia, India and Pakistan. Neil's team positively identified him as the middle man in over two hundred transactions. Most recently he was promoted to operations and was about to supervise his first attack here in the U.S."

"What was your rationale for killing him in a public park?"

Cal shrugged. "I wanted to send a message."

"You seem to be all about sending messages these days."

"What can I say? Me and Snake Eyes are pretty good."

Travis's eyes narrowed. "This isn't a game, Cal."

"Don't you think I know that? You gave me this job to take out bad guys. That's what I'm doing."

"I'm not saying you're not."

"Then what's your point?" flared Cal.

"I'm not the only one that thinks you might have lingering thoughts about Wyoming."

Cal breathed in and out slowly, willing himself to calm down. The previous October, he'd lost men, including one of his best friends, Brian Ramirez, in an operation to rescue Neil Patel. Cal had watched as a massive explosion ripped through his team. He'd later exacted revenge on the mastermind of the kidnapping, Nick Ponder.

Daniel broke the awkward silence. "I've been with Cal for every one of these takedowns, and although he sometimes likes to exhibit a little…flair, I can honestly say that he is never reckless."

"See?" said Cal.

"All right. You know I wouldn't ask if I didn't care. As your cousin I want to make sure you're okay. As your boss, I want to make sure you're not doing anything that could compromise the company."

"Don't worry. I know my limits. Besides, Daniel's the best babysitter around."

Travis finally laughed. "Okay. Enough of that." He slid the folder back in the drawer. "Back to the president. Will this be strictly a digital operation or do you need boots on the ground?"

"For now all I need is Neil and the two of us. I thought Daniel and I could take a trip and shadow the president on the road. It might give us a better idea of who the leak might be."

"Just keep me in the loop."

"No problem."

✛ ✛ ✛

After checking in with his secretary, Cal headed outside. "How about we head over and say hello to Top?" asked Cal.

Top was Marine Master Sergeant Willy Trent, a close friend of Cal's and lead hand-to-hand combat instructor at SSI. Not only was he huge, at just under seven feet in height, the outgoing black Marine was also an accomplished chef. Top Trent was someone you always wanted on your side.

Minutes later they entered SSI's gym facility. They passed through the professional grade free weights area and snuck into the observation room. Through the plate glass window a group of six SSI operators lined up against the far wall. Trent was in the middle of the wrestling mat demonstrating a grappling move on a seventh trainee. Cal and Daniel watched as he effortlessly tossed the man over his shoulder and guided him onto the mat. The quickness of the move surprised the trainee and made Cal smile.

Trent looked up and noticed Cal at the window. He waved and motioned for his friend to come join the fun.

A minute later, the big Marine was introducing Cal and Daniel to the new guys. There were curt nods and handshakes all around. Each man casually sized up the owner of SSI. Cal was used to it and kept the chit chat to a minimum. There would be time to bond with these men after they'd been better indoctrinated into the company. They were all experienced operators from each of the military branches. Unbeknownst to the warriors, Cal had approved each and every man before they'd been offered a position at SSI.

"Why don't you guys practice that toss and roll while I'm gone," said Trent. "I've gotta talk to the boss."

The operators paired up as Cal, Daniel and Trent left the sparring room and headed to one of the small offices down the adjoining hallway. It took Cal five minutes to bring Trent up to speed on what had happened in D.C. Top sipped on an oversized bottle of Powerade Zero as he listened.

Trent had been part of every major operation Cal led at SSI. Despite their differences in size and background, deep trust and respect cemented their relationship. Much like his close connection with Daniel, Cal's friendship with Trent had developed quickly. It was the Marine way when a fellow Jarhead saved your life. That had happened on multiple occasions in the past year and a half.

"How can I help?" asked Trent in his deep boom, once Cal finished with the debrief.

"Neil's handling the political investigation, so I think we're good there. As far as the attack on the vice president and first lady, I'm not sure yet. Figured something will probably break in the Secret Service's case. The president promised to keep us in the loop."

"You have a team on standby?"

"We were heading over to see Gaucho after talking to you."

Gaucho was one of SSI's most battle-hardened team leaders. A short Mexican and former Delta operator, Gaucho won the award for most eccentric man at SSI. He wore his long beard tightly braided in twin strands. Anyone who underestimated the squat soldier soon found out that the Hispanic hard-ass was smart and ruthless.

"Why don't I come with you? I haven't seen my little Mexican in a couple days," said Trent. Gaucho and Trent were two of the biggest pranksters at SSI. More often than not, their pranks targeted or involved the other.

Cal checked with the company switchboard and found out that Gaucho and his team had the urban assault house booked for the day. Trent dismissed his sweat soaked pupils and the three Marines hopped in Trent's jacked up Ford 350. It was a short drive on well-worn dirt trails. Trent pumped the latest country chart topper as they drove.

Ten minutes later, the rhythmic staccato of machine gun fire welcomed them as they approached the isolated training facility on the fringe of the compound. There was a red flag hanging flaccidly from a metal pole outside the building to indicate that the area was 'hot.' Trent turned down the radio and shut off the engine.

"Nothin' I like better than the sound of machine gun fire in the morning," said Trent as he stepped out and stretched his large frame in the crisp morning air.

As Cal led the way to the two-story structure, a voice came over the loudspeaker.

"Cease fire, cease fire."

The machine gun fire had already stopped, but it was customary for the range officer to make the announcement just as they would have done on any American military base around the world. SSI's founder, Marine Colonel Calvin Stokes, had insisted as much, and the rules still stood.

Masked and clad in black, SSI operators streamed out of the first floor entrance. Gaucho was easy to spot as the shortest of the bunch. He waved to Cal and motioned that he'd be over in a minute.

Two minutes later, Gaucho joined the small group. He'd put on an oversized black field jacket.

"Whadya say, boss? Stayin' outta trouble?"

Cal shrugged and shook Gaucho's hand, which turned into a brotherly hug. "As much as I can. You got a minute to talk?"

"Sure. What's up?"

Cal gave Gaucho the same report he'd given Trent earlier.

"So what's the plan?" Gaucho asked.

"Neil should have enough to release to the media soon. We'll see how that goes. As far as the other stuff, I want to make sure you and your boys are ready to jump if I need you."

"You know us, boss. Always ready."

Chapter 7
FBI Local Office, Birmingham, Alabama
12:16pm, December 16th

SPECIAL AGENT Steve Stricklin stepped out of the stuffy interrogation room and cracked his neck. The day was only half over and he was already tired of talking to the tight-lipped agents of the Birmingham office. He knew they were hiding something. It was in the way they looked at him with their smug eyes. It never crossed Stricklin's mind that maybe they just hated the fact that he was an Internal Affairs officer and a prick to boot.

Stricklin came from a modest upbringing and an above average high school education in Virginia. After college, he'd joined the Marines to see the world and get one step closer to his goal of running for public office. Along the way, he'd become an infantry officer and, in his mind, served honorably and faithfully. Former Marine First Lieutenant Steve Stricklin didn't stay in touch with any of the Marines he'd served with. He'd had a lofty vision of what an infantry Marine looked like: tall, muscular, square jawed and ready for war. It was what he saw when he looked in the mirror.

What he'd found had left him sickened not only for his country, but more importantly, for his own career. How was he supposed to become a top platoon commander if the Marine Corps gave him dumb farm boys from Arkansas and swamp people from Louisiana?

Two months after reporting to his battalion, Second Lieutenant Stricklin pleaded with his company commander to allow him to pick new men from incoming School of Infantry classes. The captain, a former enlisted Mustang who Stricklin had come to loathe, practically laughed him out of the office.

As was his right, 2nd Lt. Stricklin requested mast with the battalion commander for the way his own company commander, a man who was charged by the Marine Corps to mentor 2nd Lt. Stricklin, had treated him. Steve also wanted to 'suggest' to the battalion commander that maybe he be allowed to be re-assigned to another company.

The meeting had not gone as planned. With his company commander and battalion Sergeant Major looking on, the battalion commander had at first politely listened to 2nd Lt. Stricklin's tale, but had then narrowed his eyes and spoken with utter disdain.

"Who do you think you are, Lieutenant? What gives you the right to come in here and charge Captain Nanko?"

"Sir, I believe it's my right under the Uniform Code of Military Justice to—."

"That's the only reason I sat and listened to your load of crap, *Lieutenant*." The word *lieutenant* came out of the battalion commander's mouth as if he'd vomited out the vilest piece of food. "Here's what you're going to do, Lieutenant. You will officially drop these ridiculous charges of harassment, for which you have no merit, I might add, and get your candy ass back to work."

"But, sir," protested Stricklin.

"I'm not finished," growled the battalion commander. "I'm willing to keep this quiet as long as you shut your mouth and get back to what you were sent to this battalion for, getting your Marines ready for war. I'm not sure if you've heard, but we might be going over to the sandbox soon and you sure as shit better have your act together. I'll tell you something else. I regularly talk to each of my company commanders about their troops. I also talk to my Marines, private on up. I know more than you think. I've heard about you, Lieutenant. I know you like to take credit for what your Marines do. I know that you like to place blame on others."

"Sir, if you would tell me who told you these lies—."

"I told you to shut your mouth, Lieutenant. And no, I will not tell you who told me. It doesn't matter. Let's just say that once the Lance Corporal rumor mill starts up, there isn't much that can stop it. I'm willing to give you another chance, and so is Captain Nanko, as long as you start learning what it means to be a Marine officer. Despite what you might think, Lieutenant, leading Marines is a privilege, not a right."

Stricklin stood at attention in absolute shock. How could the battalion commander be so blind? Couldn't he see that he was being bullied and thrown under the bus?

"So what's it gonna be, Lieutenant?"

Stricklin hesitated, and then squared his jaw and looked straight ahead. "Sir, I'd like to respectfully request mast with the Commanding General."

The battalion commander let out a sigh and looked to Capt. Nanko, who nodded sadly.

"That's your right, Lieutenant. Sergeant Major, please provide Lieutenant Stricklin with the proper paperwork and get the general on the line for me."

The same thing had happened with the Commanding General. Stricklin still didn't understand. They'd all been against him. In the end, he'd landed in the battalion's S-3 (operations) shop where his daily routine was consumed with inspections of the battalion armory, barracks and offices. Surprisingly, he'd enjoyed the duty and took each and every detailed inspection seriously. He'd busted no fewer than fifteen Marines who were secretly drinking under age in the barracks. Over the strong objections of the Marines' platoon commanders, his own naïve peers, the battalion commander had reluctantly disciplined the minors. Instead of being praised for his hard work in the successful raid, 2nd Lt. Stricklin was reassigned to the armory, permanently.

He served out his time with relative ease, despite having to go off to war with the battalion.

The entire episode had shown Steve Stricklin that he was the only person who could and would determine his fate. With a glowing recommendation from a supply major he'd met in Saudi Arabia, Stricklin applied and was accepted to the FBI Academy. At the time, the FBI was looking for as many service members with practical experience as it could find. Although he didn't get assigned to a field office as an investigating agent as he'd originally wanted, his appointment to Internal Affairs came with certain perks. He was allowed to make his own day for the most part, and whenever he visited a field office, he was given a wide berth. Steve liked the feeling of power that it gave him.

After grabbing a soda from the staff lounge, he headed to his temporary office, a small but tidy corner office that gave him the privacy he liked. Logging in to his email, he scanned the various compartmental messages. An email from his supervisor sat waiting. Steve clicked on it.

The message contained one of his department's weekly updates that kept the entire IA team informed about ongoing investigations. Nothing peaked his interest until the update labeled *FLOTUS ORANGE BEACH, ALABAMA*. FLOTUS was the acronym used to describe the first lady of the United States. Just like the rest of Americans, Steve had heard about the attack on the first lady and the death of the vice president. The memo outlined the first lady's itinerary in Orange Beach and then asked for two volunteers to augment the investigators doing local checks prior to the first lady's appearance starting the next day. Orange Beach wasn't far from Birmingham.

Steve was surprised that the first lady was already coming out in public. Curious, he clicked on the link that took him to a secure web page where he could see if anyone had volunteered yet. There was one name. He didn't recognize the agent. His interviews in Birmingham could be finished the same day if Stricklin kept the Birmingham staff at the office until he was done, which would probably be well past midnight. They couldn't complain. It was his call to make. Even the special agent in charge of the division had to listen.

Smiling, Steve entered his name to volunteer for the temporary duty in Orange Beach. He could be there by morning.

✦ ✦ ✦

"Is everything in place?"

"Yes."

"I don't want any mistakes this time."

"There won't be."

"Good. Call me when you get to Orange Beach."

Chapter 8
En Route to Pensacola, Florida
9:05am, December 17th

CAL TRIED to stretch his legs but cuffed his shin on the seat in front him.

"Remind me why I don't book first class again."

Daniel Briggs chuckled, not looking up from the Bible he was reading. "You always say you don't want special treatment."

Cal gave Daniel an annoyed scowl and rubbed his leg. "How is it that you're not uncomfortable? You're bigger than me."

"Must be the sniper in me that got me used to squeezing and staying in the tiniest hides. This is roomy."

"You squirrely bastard."

They'd only been on the plane for a little over an hour. Daniel knew Cal's unease wasn't just about the limited legroom. His boss didn't like going into an operation blind. They were all feeling the after-effects of the deadly mission in Wyoming months before, Cal most of all. Despite the perceived recklessness of their recent assassinations where they eliminated high value targets, every mission had been meticulously planned and prepped.

The loss of his men still weighed on Cal, and Daniel knew it would take time for the feeling to diminish. It would never fully go away. Leading men into battle was dangerous. Cal was no coward, but he was human. Daniel had lost men in battle, including his best friend. He knew post-traumatic stress differed from person to person. Internally, Cal had decided that the best way to tackle his demons was to stay busy. Daniel knew it couldn't last. Everyone had a breaking point. Daniel said a silent prayer for his dead comrades and the heir of SSI. Cal needed all the help he could get and the sniper was determined to be there every step of the way.

"Any word from Neil?" Daniel asked.

"Let me check." Cal clicked on his tablet and logged into his encrypted SSI account. There was a message waiting. Cal nudged Daniel and pointed to the screen. The sniper looked down and read along with Cal.

First two stories set to break at noon EST. One donkey and one elephant as requested. Happy travels and bring me back some shrimp. NP

Cal glanced at his watch. They'd be on the ground by the time the stories broke. Cal had insisted on remaining completely neutral, ignoring political lines. The simplest way he could figure was to release two at a time, always choosing a member of each party. It wouldn't be hard to do, as Neil's list already had twenty names on it. It was pretty evenly distributed between Democrats and Republicans. Bombshells would soon be dropped all over the country.

Cal wished he'd thought of it before. It might be painful for the nation but, in Cal's mind, necessary to restore some sense of honor within the halls of Washington. Maybe in the future politicians would think twice about selling their souls. The thought of some invisible guard dog watching their every move might do the trick.

Hell, why should they be any different? The government was already spying on Americans and would soon deploy drones around the country. Shouldn't some accountability be thrown back in their faces?

+ + +

Minutes before Cal and Daniel's flight landed, two men, one tall and balding, the other of average height and build, hailed a taxi outside the Pensacola airport terminal.

"Super Six Inn on Plantation," said the larger man as he squeezed into the backseat, keeping the carry-on in his lap.

The taxi driver nodded and pulled out into the slow airport traffic.

✝✝✝

As was their routine, Daniel headed for baggage claim and Cal walked to the rental counter. Fifteen minutes later, they met up and hopped in their rented dark blue sedan. The drive to Orange Beach would take a little less than an hour, barring any traffic.

Cal turned on the radio and waited for the news to break.

Chapter 9
The White House
12:02pm, December 17th

THE PRESIDENT'S STAFF was alerted to the breaking news almost an hour before by a local NBC affiliate looking for an official comment. There was none.

The president loosened his tie, sipped on his second cup of coffee for the day and looked around the room. His Chief of Staff and National Security Adviser sat looking like bored kids waiting for a badly made science film to start in junior high, checking an endless stream of emails on their phones. Things had changed from when they'd first entered the White House. Breaking news rarely excited their now numbed nerves unless it was a possible scandal for the administration.

The president knew this news would wake them up. He'd spoken briefly with Cal prior to the Marine boarding his plane to Florida. He hadn't expected Cal's team to put something together so fast. Reminding himself never to underestimate the formidable Marine, he watched as the news unfolded on the large flat screen.

The face of the distinguished NBC anchor, Pat Landon, appeared.

Good afternoon. Breaking news from our nation's capital today. An anonymous informant approached one of our affiliates early this morning with potentially explosive evidence detailing political and corporate corruption. Our staff worked diligently to corroborate the information we received detailing the alleged misconduct by Republican Congressman Joel Erling of Colorado, and Democratic Congressman Peter Quailen of Louisiana. We were unable to obtain comments from either of the congressman's offices.

We'd like to warn you that the following video is disturbing and meant for mature audiences.

The screen changed and a jumpy video began to play.

"Put him over there, under the light," came the voice of the man behind the camera.

"You sure you want to be taping this?" came another voice from off camera.

"It'll just be my little souvenir, don't worry."

A wet slapping sound could be heard as the shot focused on a wooden chair set against a far wall. Dim light illuminated the grungy area that was littered with wooden crates and cardboard boxes.

The slapping sound stopped.

"Hurry up. I have a lunch to get to," said the person behind the camera.

A scraping sound was followed by two figures coming into view. One, a large man in a coat and slacks, dragged another man to the chair against the wall and shoved him into a half seated position. The shot focused on the bloody mess. His long hair and scruffy beard looked spotted where someone had yanked out patches that dripped blood.

The tortured man tried to speak and got a wet slap in response from the hulking figure standing next to him. Red spattered onto the wall and the guard wiped the back of his hand off on the prisoner's plaid shirt.

"That's enough," came the voice from behind the camera. "Sit him up so he can listen politely."

The gory mess of a man tried to focus on the cameraman, but his head kept lolling and swaying.

"I thought we'd had this conversation before, Jeremiah," said the cameraman's voice. "I've been working really hard for you in D.C. The least you could do is make sure you and your associates pay me on time."

"But I did..."

"You came to me, remember? You begged and begged until I finally let my staff schedule a meeting. You told me that once marijuana was legalized on the local level, my payments would triple. Why haven't I seen that extra money, Jeremiah?"

"I told you, the feds are all over my ass. They've already raided us twice."

"That's not my problem. We had an agreement. I held up my end of the bargain and pleaded your case, not only to my friends here in Colorado, but also to my colleagues on Capital Hill. Do you know how many hours I've spent fighting for your cause? Do you know how much I could be getting paid to lobby for someone else?"

Jeremiah didn't answer, hanging his head between his legs instead.

The video bobbed as the cameraman moved closer and handed the camera to his partner. Now the video showed the cameraman, attired in a form-fitting pinstripe suit and looking every bit the retired NFL lineman, approach Jeremiah and deliver a series of quick hooks that sent the victim's head snapping left and right like some macabre punching doll.

The beating stopped abruptly, the aggressor's chest heaving from the exertion, just barely.

"See what you've done? Now I'll have to go back to my office and get a new suit before my lunch with the Women's Auxiliary of Denver."

The beaten man didn't respond except to moan softly. His eyes were swollen shut from the assault.

The first cameraman turned his ruggedly handsome face to his co-conspirator and grabbed for the phone.

"Dump him back at his place. I'll meet you at the office and you can drive from there."

The TV screen switched back to the news anchor.

We have confirmed that the man you just witnessed being brutally assaulted is none other than Jeremiah Stevens, CEO of the largest legalized medical marijuana growing operation in Colorado. Our team is currently trying to locate Mr. Stevens for comment.

The last man you saw on the video appears to be Congressman Joel Erling. Once again, the congressman's office has repeatedly denied our requests for comment. We hope to have more on this soon.

The news anchor paused and nodded to someone off camera.

We know you'd all like to see what the next story is, but I've been just told by our producer that we'll need to take a quick commercial break in order to confirm an additional source's testimony. We'll be right back.

The room sat in silence, staring at the television screen that now showed a commercial for long-term health insurance.

The president's chief of staff was the first to speak. "You think that was real?"

National Security Adviser Ivan Winger nodded gravely. "I don't think there can be any doubt."

"What does this do for us?" asked the president.

His chief of staff, a tall scrawny former environmental lawyer named Rick Vance, scratched his head. "Well, I don't know if it really makes us look bad. America already thinks politicians are a bunch of criminals. I don't think Congressman Erling will be in office much longer. What I'm really worried about is what they have on our Louisiana boy. He's been co-author of more than one bill that you've endorsed in the last year. The press and Republicans will find some way to pin this back on you."

"We'll deal with it," said the president.

"But, sir..."

"I said we'll deal with it, Rick."

"Yes, sir." Rick Vance frowned as he directed his attention back to his phone. He'd missed over twenty calls.

"Anything you'd like me to do, sir?" asked Ivan Winger.

"Let's just wait and see what the second bombshell is. Can't imagine it could be much worse."

Winger shifted his focus to his own constantly buzzing phone. It was going to be another long day.

A moment later, the news returned and the second video played. It was no less shocking than the first. The recording showed Congressman Peter Quailen, naked with private parts blurred, accompanied by another nude male, purportedly the CEO of a Louisiana barge company, surrounded by eight naked women frolicking in sexual fever. Not only did the voyeuristic angle capture the carnal appetites of the two men and their partners, along with copious use of some white powdery substance that stuck stubbornly to the Congressman's red face, it also showed a rather detailed discussion where the politician promised to torpedo any and all legislation that would aid the competition of his undressed friend.

From the looks on their faces, the men sitting in the Oval Office didn't know whether to laugh or scream. The shear audacity of the act shocked them all, including the president. How could the man be so stupid?

The news anchor's face returned to the screen.

We would like to reiterate that the identities of the individuals you have just seen are still under investigation. NBC is already cooperating with FBI and White House officials to further their own analysis of the evidence provided to our offices this morning.

Coming up next, I will be interviewing former Attorney General—

The president clicked off the television and turned to his two closest advisers.

"Well, gentlemen, looks like it's going be another great day in Washington."

Chapter 10
Orange Beach, Alabama
1:26pm, December 17th

CAL COULDN'T stop his steady chuckle. They'd bounced from radio show to radio show listening to hosts and pundits talk up, over and around the new scandal. While there were a few that recommended the two congressmen be given the chance to explain, it was plain that America had already made up its mind. The politicians were guilty.

"How did Neil find that stuff?" Daniel asked as the radio station went to a commercial.

"Haven't you learned not to ask? I don't understand half the stuff he says he's doing."

"And there's no way they can trace this back to us?"

Cal shook his head. "Sounds like this was a total cakewalk. Neil said it was like strolling into an unlocked convenience store with no clerk and no security camera, and taking anything he wanted. These guys were so fucking arrogant that they led us straight to it. I can't wait until the next one."

"When?"

"I'll have to talk to the president, but I'm thinking we hit them again in a couple days."

Daniel knew nothing could ever be as easy as Cal made it sound. He just hoped that it wouldn't come back to bite them.

✛ ✛ ✛

"Where the fuck did that video come from?" boomed Congressman Peter Quailen. He'd been in the middle of a charity golf tournament when his aide called with the breaking news. Speeding home in his chauffeured Cadillac Escalade, Quailen watched in open-mouthed shock as the video played on his phone. It had been easy to find on YouTube and already had over three hundred thousand views in less than an hour.

Unlike the brazen recording made by his colleague from Colorado, Quailen knew nothing about his video. He had no way of knowing that SSI had connected the dots with the help of facial recognition and the contact list in the congressman's phone. Neil's software had dug the rest of the way.

Of course, the congressman remembered the cocaine-filled orgy that his old friend put together three years before. It had been a pre-celebration for a huge block of Post-Katrina aid Quailen pushed through Congress and was set to make his high school pal a very wealthy man.

It was that very wealthy man that was now on the other end of the call.

"I don't know, Pete. It must've been one of them hookers we got."

"Listen and listen good you fucking jackass. Don't say a thing to anyone. Let me find out what else they know and I'll be in touch. Keep your phone on!"

Quailen slammed his phone down onto the leather seat. Things were dire at the moment, but the twenty-year congressman was a veteran of more than his share of controversy. He'd risen through the ranks of Louisiana politics clawing, bribing, bullying and squashing his opponents all the way to the top.

Congressman Peter Quailen's eyes closed as he prepared a counterattack.

✦✦✦

In his posh Georgetown suite, Colorado Congressman Joel Erling was the exact opposite of his Louisiana colleague. The brash man featured in his private home video had vanished. Erling sobbed into his soiled suit coat and wriggled in his piss-soaked Armani pants.

Like other men of power, a little more than an hour ago, Erling had felt invincible. A year into his first term in Congress, he'd put out feelers to potential private 'donors.' With Colorado being a haven for marijuana growers, and with legislation already moving toward legalization, the coming crop of pot CEOs were his first target.

Through mutual friends he met Jeremiah Stevens, a kind of folk hero in the legalization movement, at a fundraiser for some children's charity. The relationship started casually with larger and larger cash payments going to Congressman Erling as his efforts in the state legislature and in Washington escalated. Erling's greed and hunger for power outmatched the pace of the bribes. He'd always been a bully as a teenager, aided by his size, and now had the added benefit of being a United States congressman. The last two years he'd lived like a movie star and even had Hollywood elites clamoring to spend time with him. He was the face of the legal marijuana movement, although he never touched the stuff himself. His vanity ran deep, and he refused any foreign substance that took away from his near perfect physique, honed from years in the gym.

He palmed the silver revolver in his hand and almost laughed at the irony. It had been a 'donor' who'd given the Congressman the weapon after a weekend of wining and dining in Los Angeles. Grabbing the pistol in his right hand, Joel Erling lifted it to his temple.

✝ ✝ ✝

Cal was just unpacking his bag when Daniel walked into the hotel room dressed in a t-shirt, running shorts and running shoes. The sniper had taken a quick jog to scope out the venue for the first lady's coming appearance. Although the run had been just over four miles, the ponytailed Marine was barely winded.

"See anything interesting?" asked Cal. He'd wanted to go along on the recon, but chose to stay back and check in with Neil back at headquarters. They'd lain out the particulars of the next two stories being leaked to the media the following week.

"There was Secret Service crawling all over the place. Helos overhead and roving patrols. They're not taking any chances."

Knowing security would be high, they'd planned accordingly. The president personally requested that Cal and Daniel be given unlimited access in and around The Amphitheatre at the Wharf, the venue for the first lady's concert. The protection detail was expecting them.

Cal appreciated the gesture, but did not want to overstay his welcome. He knew what it was like to have outsiders messing around a volatile situation. Besides, the fewer people that knew about the two Marines' movement the better. They'd make an appearance as close to the live event as possible.

"What time is the show?" Cal asked.

"The concert starts at ten tomorrow morning."

"How many people do you think they can cram in?"

The concert had been a popular draw since its inception three years earlier. With the friends the first lady fostered in Hollywood, her public events became increasingly noteworthy. At least two big music stars were always in attendance and usually singing for her benefit, free of charge. That meant big numbers.

"The venue website says ten thousand."

Cal shook his head. "Crap. Well, nobody said we were in charge of protecting her. That's the Secret Service's job. I hope they're pulling out all the stops, though. Sounds like a goat rope to me."

Daniel shrugged. To him it was just another day.

Chapter 11
Orange Beach, Alabama
4:26pm, December 17th

SPECIAL AGENT Steve Stricklin glanced over the 'hot list' the agent in charge had given him upon arrival. He'd been in town most of the day and had already interviewed eight of the ten people on the list. Nothing special so far. Just the usual weirdos and felons. Stricklin got the feeling that each and every one had been through the process before. They'd looked bored as he'd asked his canned questions.

With darkness already descending on the off-season beach town, Stricklin thought about what to do next. He could either chase down the last two guys on his list or go back to the hotel, get changed, and grab a bite to eat. The remaining suspects were probably the same as the rest and Stricklin doubted anyone would be following up to see if he'd checked on them. He could always come up with an excuse. He was good at that.

His mind made up, Stricklin flipped the assignment sheet over to where the Secret Service and FBI contacts were listed for the event. Below the switchboard phone number was another list of outside authorities given high-level access to the site. Most were local law enforcement officials. Stricklin's eyes stopped on the fifth name on the list: *Calvin Stokes, Jr.* It couldn't be the same guy. The only Calvin Stokes he knew had served as one of his very first squad leaders in the Marine Corps. He still remembered how his company commander had bragged about Sergeant Stokes. "You need anything done pronto, you give it to Stokes, Steve. That kid is sharp. Take care of him."

Lt. Stricklin had tried to do just that. When they'd first met, like any good infantry officer, he'd outlined his philosophy and stressed the point that he was in command. He'd made it plain that enlisted Marines were beneath him, not just in rank, but also as men. Stokes hadn't said much in that first meeting, but had said plenty in the months to come. In Stricklin's eyes, Sgt. Stokes had gone rogue by leading the coup that had eventually seen the platoon commander shipped to S-3.

No, it couldn't be the same person. Stricklin figured that the Stokes he knew had probably been killed in Iraq or ended up in the Portsmouth brig. Regardless, he circled the contact number next to Calvin Stokes, Jr. and promised to call the VIP later.

Heading back to his hotel room to get changed, he scanned the strip for a decent place to eat.

+ + +

Daniel led the way into the local restaurant. The smell of fried seafood greeted them as they opened the door. As was his duty, Daniel glanced around the dining room before motioning Cal in. He made it look like a casual diner checking out a new eatery, but the sniper had actually mentally noted all entrances and dark spots in the room. He took his collateral duty of bodyguard very seriously. Cal knew better than to object.

A pretty blond hostess walked toward them in tight cutoff jeans and a red t-shirt provocatively tied in the front. She glanced at the two Marines and smiled seductively.

"Just the two of y'all, or are your girlfriends coming?" she asked.

"Just us," said Cal with a smile.

The young girl's grin widened at the prospect of wooing the two good-looking diners.

"Why don't y'all follow me." She grabbed two menus and a small stack of napkin-wrapped silverware. "I'll get you a seat with a view."

It turned out that the only view the two Marines would have for the night was the flirty hostess who flitted by whenever she wasn't seating customers or helping bus tables.

Cal nursed a beer and Daniel sipped an unsweetened ice tea as they waited for their food. The place was packed and the din of the other customers easily masked their conversation. They'd managed to finalize their plans for the following day when Cal's face reddened.

"No fucking way," Cal said through gritted teeth.

"What?"

Cal looked down at the table and slouched, minimizing his silhouette. "That guy that just walked in by the bar," Daniel casually looked over his shoulder. A good-looking man stood waiting for the hostess. He was wearing a linen shirt over crisply creased khakis.

"You know him?"

Cal nodded and chugged the rest of his beer. "Steve Stricklin. He was one of my platoon commanders. Fucking asshole."

Before Daniel could probe, the unwanted intruder locked eyes on Cal.

"Shit," grimaced Cal.

Marching over like he was on the parade deck, Stricklin stepped up to the table.

"Good evening, Stokes."

With a tone laced with contempt, Cal replied, "Hello, Steve."

"I can't say I'm surprised to see you here. This must be your friend Mr. Briggs."

Cal and Daniel's heads whipped around.

"How did you know that?" Cal snapped.

Stricklin smirked at Cal's discomfiture. "I'm with the FBI now."

"What does that have to do with us?" asked Cal.

"You're on a watch list that hit my desk today," said Stricklin. He grinned. "I thought I'd stop by and make sure you were staying out of trouble."

Cal moved to stand and confront the man. Daniel grabbed his arm and shook his head. Cal glared at his friend and forced himself to take a deep breath.

"We were actually just leaving," said Cal, turning to face Stricklin. Daniel withdrew a fifty-dollar bill and laid it on the table.

"I'll be seeing you around, Stokes."

Without another word, Daniel followed Cal out the back door of the restaurant..

+ + +

Cal hadn't said a thing as he marched his way back to their rental and taken off. He drove, gripping the steering wheel with white knuckles.

"You wanna tell me what that was all about?" asked Daniel.

Cal grumbled something under his breath and exhaled. "The last time I saw Lieutenant Stricklin, the guy was hiding under a folding table covered in C rations while the Taliban lobbed mortars at the CP. I happened to be there with Andy as his acting platoon sergeant. (Andy, now Capt. Bartholemew Andrews, was one of Cal's best friends, former platoon commander and fellow Navy Cross winner.) While me and Andy ran around helping the headquarters staff call in a counter battery strike, Lieutenant Stricklin hid under that fucking table shitting his pants."

"How'd he end up in the FBI?"

"I have no fucking idea. The bigger question is how he found out about us. I don't want that prick on my ass. He's all about stepping on others to advance his career. I can't wait to tell Andy about this." Cal shook his head, still in disbelief over the sighting.

Capt. Andrews was currently stationed at Eighth & I with the Marine Corps Silent Drill Team. Cal had repeatedly offered his old friend a position at SSI, but the salty Marine always politely declined, saying his time in the Corps wasn't up yet.

Cal was sure that Andy would be a general some day. That was if he could put up with the bullshit and the career-builders that seemed to cling to the Corps like babies on a teat. They'd had numerous conversations about the talent exodus after officers attained the rank of captain. A rock star officer had the option of either leaving for a good job in the civilian world or sticking it out in a Marine Corps that was increasingly political and notorious for riding good officers and enlisted Marines until they broke.

"Is Andy still at Eighth and I?" asked Daniel.

"Yeah. I think his time's about up. He should be heading back to The Fleet soon. He'll make a great company commander, if I can't convince him to join us."

Daniel smiled. He might've been the same as Andy if it hadn't been for his PTSD and the 'almost' Medal of

Honor. SSgt Daniel Briggs was considered a shoe-in for the nation's highest award until the president stopped the process. Unknown to all but Daniel, Cal and the president, it had been Daniel who'd personally requested he not receive the medal. The president couldn't really refuse since Daniel had just been part of the team who saved the president's life.

Like Cal, Daniel still loved the Marine Corps. Unlike Cal, if things had been different, Daniel might now be Gunnery Sergeant Daniel Briggs. It didn't matter now. He was at peace with his decision. More than that, he was happy being part of the SSI family.

"I don't know if you'll have much luck getting him out, Cal."

"I know. He's a hard-headed knuckle-dragger."

Both Marines laughed.

"What do you want to do about this Stricklin guy?"

Cal's smile disappeared. "Let me think about it. Unfortunately, I think Lady Luck just shat in our Cheerios. I'm pretty sure the president's call to the Secret Service got us on some list."

"And then serendipity gave Stricklin access to that list," finished Daniel. "You think we can call the president and get this guy off our tail?"

"I think the president has enough to worry about. Let's just play it by ear. Maybe Stricklin's just some flunky. Who knows? Maybe he's lying just to antagonize me. I wouldn't put it past him. Why don't you text Neil and have him access the guy's file from the Marine Corps and FBI databases. I want to know what we're dealing with. I'm also curious about why he's down here."

As Cal drove the rest of the way back to the hotel, Daniel sent the requested information to Neil Patel.

At almost the same moment Steve Stricklin was sending a similar request to FBI headquarters regarding Calvin Stokes, Jr. and Daniel Briggs.

✝ ✝ ✝

"What do you mean I can't have the files?" Stricklin asked angrily into the phone.

"They're tagged above your access level, sir," responded the after-hours FBI dispatcher.

Stricklin had tried unsuccessfully to access anything about Cal or Daniel. After hitting a wall, he'd called the Hoover Building. Something wasn't right with the situation. He'd never been denied access to records. Well, except for that one time he'd tried to dig into an old supervisor's personal file. He'd received a verbal warning for that.

"Let me see who I can get on the line. I'll call you back."

Stricklin killed the call. What was Stokes up to?

✝ ✝ ✝

Neil had all the information Cal needed by the time he and Daniel walked into their shared room with a bag of half-eaten fast food. They had SSI's tech genius on speaker phone.

"You're not gonna believe this, Cal. This guy tried accessing both of your records."

Cal glared at the phone. "Did he get in?"

"Who do you think I am?" came Neil's exasperated voice. "Of course he didn't get in. I wrapped them up tight."

"I thought you'd already taken care of that," said Cal.

There was moment's silence. It wasn't often that someone got around Neil's tricks.

"I hadn't really taken into account that someone from their Internal Affairs Division might want to see our files. IA agents get more access. What's this guy got against you anyway?"

"It's a long story. Did you find out why he's down here?"

"Yeah. Looks like it's just dumb luck. He volunteered to augment the Bureau's pre-event investigation staff. He left Birmingham last night after a couple days hammering the local agents about some whistleblower claim."

"Why do you think he volunteered?" Daniel asked.

"I'll send you his personnel record, but I think it's to be around VIPs, or maybe just to chill at the beach. From what I was able to scan of his profile assessment, this Stricklin guy is a real piece of work. You should see the things the FBI psychologist called him. Bet you a million bucks he wanted to pick up chicks at the beach and stand next to the first lady."

"That sounds like Stricklin," growled Cal. "Any way you can get this guy reassigned?"

"When's the event?"

"Ten tomorrow morning."

"If I had a little more time, maybe. I could drop a note to a couple of our contacts..."

"Don't worry about it. I don't want you to waste your time on this guy," said Cal. "We'll take care of him if he becomes a problem."

"You're not thinking about..." Neil started.

"I'm not that stupid, Neil. We'll just avoid the guy."

"Oh. Okay." Neil sounded relieved. He was one of a small cadre within SSI that knew what Cal and Daniel had been doing over the preceding months, namely killing people quietly.

"Did you send over Stricklin's file?" asked Cal.

"I did. Let me know if you need anything else."

Cal asked about the progress of what Neil had dubbed Operation Pest Control. The two Marines listened to Neil's report, thanked him, and ended the call.

"You need me?" Daniel asked.

"No. Why don't you go to bed? I'll scan through this stuff on Stricklin. I won't be up long."

"Wake you at zero five?"

"Yeah."

As Daniel got ready for bed, Cal read Stricklin's file. Memories came rushing back from his time in the Marine Corps. To those uneducated in Marine lingo and performance review, Stricklin's record would seem satisfactory, if not above average. There were, however, indirect ways for reviewing officers to insert traits like 'indecisive' and comments like 'more training suggested in X area,' or the absence of a 'recommended for promotion' that were red flags to those in the know. Cal wasn't surprised to see Stricklin's fitness reports peppered with such subtle verbiage. To someone like Cal, Stricklin's entire Marine Corps personnel file, minus the mind-boggling recommendation from some major, screamed "SHITTY OFFICER."

Cal wasn't as familiar with the FBI ranking system, and yet he saw similar currents of politically correct wording used to describe Special Agent Steve Stricklin's performance. If he hadn't been so annoyed at Stricklin's appearance, Cal might have laughed at the private evaluation by the FBI shrink that Stricklin had never been given access to. It included words like conniving, self-aggrandizing, calculating and sub-par.

If he'd had time, he would have sent the evals to SSI's resident head examiner Dr. Higgins for advice on how to handle the FBI agent. A former lead CIA interrogator and psychiatrist, the portly doctor was the best Cal had ever met. That was saying a lot considering Cal's usual distrust for 'non-medical' doctors.

Finished with his perusal, Cal stowed his laptop and hurried to get ready for bed. He was sure that one way or another, the next day would be interesting.

Chapter 12
Orange Beach, Alabama
6:03am, December 18th

"**DON'T WORRY**, honey, I'll be fine. Yes, Jerry says everything's taken care of." The first lady paused to listen to her husband's third protest and nodded to the head of her protection detail. "I told you, I'm not going to let these murderers stop me from helping the American people. Aren't you the one always saying that we should continue living our lives despite attacks?" She smiled at the president's reply.

"I love you too. Don't worry, I'll get you and the girls a couple autographs. We'll call after the event. Bye, honey."

The first lady put down the secure phone and looked up at her security detail. There were four male and one female Secret Service agents waiting patiently.

"Everything okay, ma'am?" Jerry Laskin, the head of her detail, asked. He'd been with her for three years and they'd developed a good working relationship.

"Just fine, Jerry. You know the president, always worried about me."

"I think this time he has reason to be worried," said Jerry, pointing down at the hot pink bandage on the first lady's leg.

"For the last time, I'm fine." The slightest hint of annoyance crossed her face, but was instantaneously covered by her signature smile. "Is everything ready?"

"Yes, ma'am. We've got the extra teams doing another sweep and the supplemental x-ray machines just arrived. I'm about to run over and take a look at them."

"What about the crowd? Is there a line yet?"

"Around the block. The local PD has the sidewalks roped off."

"Good. I don't want anyone getting run over. Please do everything you can to ensure the event runs smoothly." It wasn't a request. It was an order.

The first lady walked back into the hotel bedroom to finish getting ready.

"You two stay here," Laskin said to the bald male agent and the gruff female agent. "I'll be back before she leaves." He pointed to where the first lady had disappeared.

As the eighteen-year Secret Service veteran left the room, he said a silent prayer that the concert go off without a hitch. He'd been off-duty the day of the attack at the Air and Space Museum. He wasn't going to be farther than ten feet from the first lady anytime she stepped in public for as long as he was in charge.

✚ ✚ ✚

6:00am

Cal and Daniel left the hotel in a cab, not wanting to have the hassle of finding parking. Worst case they could walk back. It was something they'd done plenty of times in the Corps.

The driver dropped them off two blocks from the amphitheater. Four minutes later they checked in with the Secret Service agent manning a side gate. It didn't hurt that they were on the list. After putting on their lanyards holding their all-access security badges, the two Marines entered the venue and began their inspection.

✚ ✚ ✚

6:51am

"You ready, Mikey?" The man in a fluorescent blue tank top with a sailfish on the front asked his companion.

"Yeah." The other man, wearing a pair of board shorts and a white t-shirt that said, 'Redneck & Proud,' rubbed his stomach like it was bothering him. "Let me take another shit before we start walkin'."

"Fuck. That's yer third one this mornin'. What's wrong with you?"

"Don't know. I'll be right back."

After a fair bit of groaning, and another flush, Mikey emerged.

"You light a match?"

"Shut up. Let's go." The man's face was drawn and pale. Sweat beaded heavily on his brow.

"You don't look so good."

"I said shut up."

The sick man's cohort grunted and led the way out.

+ + +

8:00am

The amphitheater opened its doors to the swarm of patrons. A steady stream of concert-goers passed through one of many metal detectors or x-ray machines. Some were chosen at random for more invasive searches. Most were somber and respectful, aware of the heightened presence of security personnel after the attack that injured the first lady and killed the vice president.

Much of the crowd looked to be from out of town, which wasn't uncommon for the occasion. The typical fans for the artists performing were more left-leaning than right. The citizenry of Orange Beach was comprised of mostly southern conservatives, a group not known for their adoration of the first lady and her Hollywood friends.

There were, of course, exceptions. Some came merely to see the first lady and her entourage of celebrities. Others came because of curiosity. It helped that the event was heavily subsidized and most tickets could be purchased for as little as fifteen dollars.

Cal and Daniel watched the mass as they meandered in and found their seats. They'd talked to most of the security team and agreed that the location was as secure as it was going to get. There was always added danger in an open air event, but the prior attack in D.C. proved that it could happen anywhere.

"You getting that tingly vibe of yours?" asked Cal.

Daniel had a sixth sense for danger. He could sniff it out like he had a direct line to a higher power. It often elicited a friendly ribbing from the other SSI operators because they all knew of his quiet, yet strong, religious faith.

Daniel shook his head. "I can't believe the president is letting her do this. They're just asking for trouble."

Cal shrugged. He'd tried to dissuade the president as recently as the night before, but it wasn't to be. Despite his reservations, the president had deferred to his wife and her security team. "She's in good hands, Cal," he'd said. "Besides, won't you be looking out for her too?"

It wasn't Cal's job to look out for the first lady, but like any good Marine, he took his marching orders with a dutiful, "Yes, sir."

As was their manner, the Marines silently observed the growing throng, ready for anything.

+ + +

9:10am

Mikey had perked up during the walk to the concert, likely due to the copious amounts of alcohol consumed from the tiny bottles of liquor his partner had stashed in every conceivable place on his person.

Both men were sporting soothing buzzes as they passed through the metal detectors. The shot-sized bottles of booze had all been consumed and thrown away prior to hitting the checkpoint. Neither man set off the alarm and the agents inspecting didn't see the need for additional screening.

+ + +

9:28am

The Secret Service suburban pulled up to the curb. Agents arranged themselves around the vehicle and along the path leading into the amphitheater's holding area. The first lady, looking elegant yet modern in a form-fitting knee length linen periwinkle dress, stepped out the SUV and smiled at the large agent offering her his hand.

"I'm fine, thank you," she smiled warmly, gingerly lowering herself onto the pavement. Her recent wounds were still raw, but the painkillers had helped.

"Right this way, ma'am." The first lady followed, encircled by her detail.

✛✛✛

9:31am

Daniel nudged Cal. "Here she comes."

They watched as the first lady took in the open air arena, pointing and waving to fans as she moved slowly across the stage.

✛✛✛

9:32am

Mikey watched as the first lady made her pre-event rounds. He even waved and forced a smile despite the aching pain in his stomach.

+++

10:00am

The crowd roared as the first lady stepped out with four of the country's biggest stars, who smiled and waved, deferring to their host as she stepped up to the microphone.

"Good morning, everyone!" The masses roared back in glee. "I'm so glad you could make it today. As you can see," the hostess pointed to her leg with a wince, "I'm on the mend, but I wouldn't miss this for the world." Another excited roar. "In case you don't recognize my friends here, let me introduce you to…"

+ + +

10:04am

Special Agent Stricklin finagled a last minute entrance to the event by flashing his FBI badge and threatening a lowly security guard with an investigation. He'd somehow made it to the far side of the venue, wanting to get a clear view of the place.

Stokes wasn't making any attempt to stay hidden. He was clearly visible from Stricklin's position. "What is he up to?" Stricklin asked.

"What's that?" a scantily clad coed yelled back to him, batting her eyes.

Scowling, Stricklin pulled out his badge and shoved it in the poor girl's face. She paled and turned to get closer to the stage.

✚ ✚ ✚

10:07am

The first act, a popular soul singer, was just winding up on stage. Soothing melodies wafted over the crowd, hushing their cheers and enducing a hypnotic swaying.

Cal ignored the singer. His eyes continued to scan the crowd, looking for anything unusual.

"See anything?"

"No." The sniper's eyes swept the throng with practiced precision. If anyone could find an attacker, it was Daniel.

"Keep looking."

✚ ✚ ✚

10:10am

Mikey did his best to move with the crowd. They'd been inching closer and closer to stage. Most people let them pass, but scowled disapprovingly when they saw who was moving through.

The nausea returned and Mikey grabbed his friend's arm to steady himself.

"You okay?"

"Yeah. Just got bumped is all."

"I still can't believe you wanted to come to this thing. You in love with the president's wife or something?"

Mikey flashed a weak grin. "Naw. Just wanted to see if you were turning into a liberal Nancy."

His friend laughed and turned back to the stage. Mikey grimaced and and fell forward.

+ + +

10:12am

Burly security guards hopped over the short barricade and moved to the man lying on the ground. "Are you okay, sir?" one of the guards yelled over the music.

Mikey was writhing on the ground, his friend kneeling down to see what he could do.

"Go get my medicine," Mikey said so only his companion could hear.

"Right now? Where is it?"

"Back in our room," he motioned for his buddy to come closer. "Stay there until after." Mikey's eyes burned with intensity. His friend nodded and backed away, turning to the guards, who were having a hard time holding the curious crowd back. "I, uh, have to run and get his medicine."

The head guard reached down to start moving the sick man. "We'll take him to the first aid station. You can pick him up there."

Mikey's friend moved off to find the nearest exit. His friend looked bad. He hoped the medicine would help.

+ + +

10:15am

Cal had watched the scene from afar. It looked like someone had had too much to drink. The troop of security guards had finally loaded the prostrate man onto a yellow stretcher and were easing their way through the crowd. He'd seen the friend leave moments earlier and had ordered a reluctant Daniel to follow him.

Now alone, Cal watched as the guards moved, keeping his eyes glued to the passage.

+ + +

10:16am

"Shit." The man observing the medical extraction from half a mile away put down his telescopic lens and pulled a cell phone out of his pocket. The redneck had passed out early. A number flashed onto the screen. He pressed DIAL.

Three seconds later, a *BOOM* sounded from the arena. The man calmly palmed the phone, threw it into the waterway below, made his way to the ground floor of the rented home and slid into the waiting car.

Chapter 13
Orange Beach, Alabama
10:18am, December 18th

THE SEMI-RETIREE looked up from his newspaper. The man with a neatly trimmed grey hair and goatee sat nursing a coffee and mild hangover looking forward to a day of cruising the deserted coast on his black 2002 Fatboy Harley Davidson. He'd polished his baby up the night before.

The explosion was close. He knew the area well. He'd lived in Orange Beach for years and had either ridden or stumbled through most of its roadways and byways. The amphitheater was ten blocks from his one bedroom condo.

He'd heard about the first lady's visit, as had anyone who read or watched the news in the off-season beach town. Not that he cared other than to grumble about the increased traffic on the normally barren streets. A familiar prickle flitted up his neck. It had never failed to warn him of danger.

More curious than concerned, Maynor slipped on his black leather riding vest with Leathernecks U.S.M.C and an eagle, globe and anchor emblazened in Marine Corps red and yellow on the back, pocketed his Colt 1911 and slipped the sheathed Kabar into the back of his waistband.

A minute later, his motorcycle rumbled to life, and Maynor headed toward the mayhem.

+ + +

Cal was lucky to have been on the opposite side of the stage. Still, he was thrown back by the force of the explosion. Ears ringing, heart pounding, the Marine moved toward the chaos. Blood and body parts littered the stage. He'd seen it before, but the absolute devastation of human life sickened him. However, unlike most people, it angered him to action.

He pushed past three of the four Hollywood heavyweights who stood with gore-splattered faces, staring down at their companion, the soul singer, whose head sat split in half by a piece of debris. Cal jumped off the stage nearly slipping on what looked like a woman's bloody stump of a hand.

The epicenter of the blast was clear. Screaming and moaning concert-goers crawled in no general direction.

Cal was joined by two Secret Service agents, who were similarly deafened by the blast.

"Is the first lady safe?" Cal bellowed.

Both of the agents nodded like robots, their normally stoic faces wide-eyed. It had happened on their watch, again. Cal could read the implications in their look.

"Where is she?" Cal asked.

One of the suited agents pointed over his shoulder. "They took her away in the helo."

Good, thought Cal. One less thing to worry about.

"Hey!" Cal had to yell again to get their attention. Their heads snapped around. "Start triaging the wounded, I'll..." Just then he felt a buzzing in his pocket. He pulled out his cell phone. It was Daniel.

"Yeah?" he answered.

He couldn't hear a damn thing, so instead he said, "Text it to me, Briggs. My ears are shit right now."

Turning back to the agents, Cal moved to help a woman who'd lost both arms and was silently screaming in pain. "Dammit," mumbled Cal.

✝ ✝ ✝

Daniel couldn't text. He was on the heels of the guy he'd followed from the arena, and who had jammed into a sprint after the explosion. At least Cal was safe. He trusted his boss and instead focused on running faster.

The guy had a good lead. Daniel, as was his fashion, said a silent prayer that his abilities not fail.

Suddenly, out of the corner of his peripheral vision, Daniel's prayer was answered. A motorcycle roared around the corner and a smile spread across Daniel's face at the sight of the Marine emblem on the rider's jacket.

"Marine!" he yelled at the rider, who quickly caught up to Daniel.

"Need a ride?" said the rider, as he pulled up alongside the sprinting sniper.

Daniel nodded and jumped onto the back of the Harley, shaking his head. *Send in the Marines*, he thought, saying thanks to the Almighty once again.

+ + +

Steve Stricklin saw Cal's friend sneak out of the concert. On a hunch, he followed at a safe distance. Minutes later, the explosion had rocked the surrounding area. Stricklin looked back, contemplating going to help, but thought better of it. He didn't want anything to do with another attack. Too much mess. Too much paperwork. Stricklin didn't have the strongest stomach. He'd once wretched at the sight of two decapitated Iraqi soldiers after a particularly brutal battle.

No. Maybe Cal's buddy knew something. Maybe he, Special Agent Steve Stricklin, could intercept the culprit. Visions of glory followed him as he commandeered a vehicle to shadow the two men on the motorcycle.

+ + +

Daniel and the motorcycle driver caught up to the running man quickly. As if it was something he'd practiced before, the biker extracted his pistol, revved up next to the runner, and delivered a vicious blow to the man's neck. The momentum of the swing and the motorcycle sent the man sprawling.

Daniel hopped off and drew his own weapon, taking a bead on the man struggling to rise. "Stay down!" ordered Daniel.

"You need help, kid?" asked the Harley rider, who was even now stepping up next to Daniel, his weapon also aimed at the struggling suspect.

"Yeah. Thanks for the help. Marine?"

"Former Lance Corporal Don Maynor at your service."

Daniel didn't have time to respond because another voice sounded from behind them. "Drop your weapons and get on the ground!"

+ + +

Stricklin couldn't believe his luck. Not only had he caught up to the Cal's pal, he'd also caught the man and his new companion unaware.

"I said, drop your weapons and get on the ground!" he yelled, a bit louder.

"I can't do that, sir," said Daniel. "This man is a suspect in the attack."

Stricklin inched closer, wary of the two men with pistols extended. He noticed the Marine logo on the motorcycle rider's back and scowled. It looked to him like a bit of a redneck gathering. Maybe he could bust all three.

"I am an FBI agent," Stricklin started.

"Let me guess, Johnny Utah?" Maynor asked, lacing his voice with sufficient sarcasm to make Daniel smile.

"Excuse me? No, *I am* Special Agent Stricklin..."

The voice and the named clicked for Daniel. "Sir, we met last night. My name is Briggs. I'm a friend of..."

"I know who you are, *Marine*." He said Marine like he was saying a word that disgusted him, stepping the final feet to stand behind Briggs and Maynor. "For the last time, drop your..."

Before he could utter another syllable, Maynor swung around and swept the butt of his pistol across Stricklin's temple. The cocky agent hit the pavement, unconscious.

Daniel barely moved. "I guess I should say you shouldn't have done that, but..."

"But the guy's an asshole, I know," finished Maynor. "Come on. We better get this other guy loaded and get the hell out of here. I don't wanna be around when Special Agent Utah wakes up. He might try to throw more *Point Break* lines at us."

The Marine sniper chuckled and moved to secure their prisoner. Maynor checked to see that Stricklin was still breathing. He was, although he'd have a nasty headache for a day or two. Maynor didn't care. He had a feeling the kid with the blond ponytail would take care of any hassles the prick agent might concoct.

+ + +

Sirens and blaring lights welcomed them back to the arena as Maynor pulled the overloaded Harley up to the curb. The smell of carnage and destruction led them inside. "I'm sorry, gentlemen, but you can't come in here," said a portly local cop.

Daniel flashed his ID badge and stepped around the barricade, dragging his suspect along by the wrists. It wasn't hard to find Cal, although his appearance made Daniel hesitate. His hair plastered his head in sweat, and his shirt and trousers were covered in darkening blood. Cal waved them over.

"Who are these guys?" asked Cal, pointing.

"Prisoner and Marine," answered Daniel. Cal looked the two up and down.

"You know how to keep your mouth shut, Marine?" Cal asked, scowling.

"Does a bear shit in the woods?" replied Maynor, meeting Cal's stare with equal intensity.

Despite the situation, Cal grinned. "Okay. We've got a Secret Service helo picking us up in ten, then Trav has a plane waiting at the airport. I think you better come along, Mister..."

"Maynor. Don Maynor."

Cal nodded. "Welcome to the clusterfuck, Maynor."

Chapter 14
Enroute to Reagan National
11:42am, December 18th

A SURLY Secret Service agent had almost prevented their departure from the arena. "I can't let you take these men with you, sir. My orders are to take yourself and Mr. Briggs. No one said a thing about the other two."

Cal might normally sympathize with the agent's predicament, but at the moment, covered in gore, head pounding and throat parched, the Marine was in no mood. "How about I get the president on the line and tell him you're obstructing *his* investigation?"

The agent's eyebrows raised. He'd been told by his superiors to give Stokes and Briggs every accommodation. That meant the order had originated from the president or one of his staff. Instead of fighting it, he ushered the four men onto the helicopter.

Less than ten minutes later, they touched down at Pensacola Naval Air Station, escorts in tow. A Gulfstream waited, and Cal didn't waste a second saying thank you. Instead he hopped out and led the way to their next ride.

Once they'd secured the prisoner to one of the leather chairs in the front row, Cal pulled out his phone. "Sir, it's Stokes. Yes, sir. We're on our way. No, sir. I think they can take care of it. We'll see you soon." Cal ended the call.

"The president says the first lady's fine. A little shaken, of course, but okay. You wanna tell me this guy's story?" he asked, pointing at the bloody-faced detainee.

Daniel ran through the story of the chase, included Stricklin's miraculous appearance.

"Fucking prick," grumbled Cal, going to run his fingers through his hair, then stopping when he remembered the gore on his hands.

"Hey, I don't mean to interrupt, but where the hell are we going?" asked Maynor, more curious than worried. "I left my bike back at the amphitheater."

"D.C. We need to brief the president. You're along for the ride now. Besides, I don't want Stricklin getting his hands on you. I'll deal with him." By the look in Cal's eyes, Maynor didn't doubt it.

One thing nagged. "How can I help?" asked Maynor.

"You guys ever use the term Semper Gumby back in your day?"

Maynor nodded with a smile.

"Semper Gumby, Maynor. Semper Fucking Gumby."

+ + +

They couldn't pry much out of the man, whose name turned out to be William "Billy" Ingersol. Billy was a third generation moonshiner from outside Montgomery, Alabama. He and the exploding man, Michael "Mikey" Lincoln, had been friends since kindergarten.

"I swear I didn't know nothin'," pleaded Billy, tears punctuating his statement. "Mikey said he wanted to go to the show. I thought he was fucking crazy, but he paid for everything, even the place we stayed at."

"You said he wasn't feeling well this morning. Do you remember how long he'd been like that?" Cal questioned.

Billy shook his head. "We hadn't hung out in a while. He got a job drivin' semis a few months back. He called me a week ago about the concert and we drove down yesterday. Mikey started complainin' this mornin', I swear."

Cal stared at the scared man. If the guy had anything to do with the attack, he didn't give a hint. "Look. Your buddy Mikey blew himself up, killing a lot of people and almost killing the first lady. I won't sugar coat it for you. Life's gonna suck for all of us for the next few weeks."

"Oh, God!" Billy's head thumped forward as his chin hit his chest, heaving with sobs.

Cal motioned to the back of the plane. Daniel and Maynor followed.

"What do you, think?" Cal asked Daniel.

"Sounds like he's telling the truth. You think someone surgically implanted a IED in his friend's stomach?"

"No fucking way," whispered Maynor.

Cal nodded. "Just like they're doing in the Middle East. Animals. We need to find out who's behind it. Let's send what we've got to the Secret Service. CC Neil on it too, and have him start digging."

+ + +

Stricklin woke to a splitting headache and a stray dog licking his face. Pushing himself up to his hands and knees, he tried to piece together what had happened. Blurry. His focus had been on the Marine with the blond hair when...the memory faded as his consciousness threatened to give way again. Instead, he convulsed, head flying forward, vomiting on the pavement, retching until all the contents from his stomach lay pooled on the ground.

Cold sweat sprouted on his face as he rose shakily to his feet, patting his pockets, looking for his cell phone. He finally found it, shattered, ten feet away.

Stumbling out of the alleyway, he made his way to the car he'd commandeered earlier.

✛ ✛ ✛

"Are you sure you're okay?" The president asked his wife, who was on a flight back to D.C. aboard an MV-22 Osprey, part of VMM-263 out of MCAS New River, North Carolina, but who'd happened to have a contingent in Pensacola for training. They were about to drop the first lady and her security in Birmingham where a faster mode of transport sat waiting.

"For the last time, I'm fine. Please focus on the dead and wounded. Oh, God, if you could have seen..."

"Try not to think about it. We've got everyone working on it, Secret Service, FBI, NSA," soothed the president. He could hear the first lady sniffling, wishing he could hold her, comfort her.

"Do you have any leads? Anything?" Her voice cracked as she asked.

The president hesitated. He didn't want to give his wife false hope. "We have a team headed back here now. They may have a witness."

"I want to be there." Her intensity flared through the phone.

"Honey, I don't think that's—."

"No. This was my concert. Those were *my* people."

The president exhaled, knowing he was in a no-win situation. "I'll see what I can do."

+ + +

"I think that's a really bad idea, sir." Cal sat, eyes closed, shaking his head. "Yes, sir. We'll see you soon."

Cal slammed the phone down and cursed under his breath.

"What happened?" asked Daniel.

It took Cal a moment to answer. He didn't want to snap at his friend. "The president *and* the first lady are meeting us at the airport. He says she wanted to be there when they question Billy." He motioned to the front of the plane, where their prisoner slept fitfully. They'd finally had to sedate him for fear of him having a nervous breakdown, or worse. "I say we drop him off, then make our way back to the house in Arlington." SSI kept a modest home, sort of a safe house, close to the capitol in case employees had to stay overnight. Mostly it was used by SSI staff taking their families sight-seeing in the nation's capitol. Cal had already checked, and no one was using it.

"How about you? You gonna get cleaned up before we see the president?" Daniel asked, pointing at his boss's blood-crusted clothing.

Cal looked down as if he'd forgotten his appearance. "I'm going like this. If they can't take it..."

Maynor whistled. "You've got some balls, brother."

Cal leveled him with a stare. The glare softened into a grin. "Semper Fi."

✚ ✚ ✚

Escorted by what looked like half the Secret Service, and a hefty police contingent, the president rolled into Reagan National Airport, effectively shutting down all traffic. Minutes later, he met the first lady's plane as it taxied to the secluded gate. He rushed up the stairs before his cadre of agents could react, and found his wife with a mascara-streaked face rising to deplane. Enveloping her in a tight embrace, he whispered, "I'm so glad you're okay."

Suddenly realizing the eyes around them, they parted and kissed chastely. "Is the witness here yet?" asked the first lady.

"They'll be here in a few minutes. We're meeting them inside."

✚ ✚ ✚

Five minutes later, the Gulfstream touched down and taxied to the spot vacated by the First lady's transport. Billy was still passed out, so Cal instructed the interrogation team sent by the Secret Service to carry him out. Cal's team debarked, finding a platoon of black clad operators waiting on the tarmac.

More than one man stared at Cal, who looked like he'd just stepped out of a horror movie. Ignoring the looks, Cal followed the lead agents into the terminal outpost.

+ + +

"Jesus," exclaimed the president as Cal walked in.

"I'm sorry for my appearance, sir, but—."

The president waved the apology away. "Thanks for coming so quickly. I take it that the man they just carried in is the witness?"

Cal hesitated, looking around the small room where over twenty staffers and assorted agents stood listening. "Can we talk somewhere private, sir?"

The president nodded, motioning for one of the agents to lead the way. Once tucked safely into a small conference room down the hallway, Cal filled the president in on what they'd gleaned from the friend of the bomber.

"You don't think he knows anything?" asked the president, obviously skeptical.

"I'm sure your guys can do a much better job interrogating him than I can, but he seemed genuinely surprised, and scared. Has the Secret Service or the FBI come up with anything?"

"No. They haven't found..."

The first lady burst into the room, frantic. "Where is he? Where is the man they brought in?" Her gaze stopped on blood-soaked Cal.

"Honey, you remember Cal Stokes. He's the Marine you met..."

"You didn't answer my question," she pressed. "Where is *that* man?"

Cal placed a hand on the president's arm. "Ma'am, we had to sedate him on the way up here. They're waiting for him to come out of it now."

The first lady looked like she wanted to say something, but burst into tears instead. Her husband quickly wrapped her in his arms. He looked over his shoulder at Cal. "Whatever you need, Cal. Find out who did this."

Cal nodded and left the room.

Chapter 15
SSI Safehouse, Arlington, VA
3:35pm, December 18th

AFTER THROWING HIS ruined clothes in the trashcan and taking a much needed shower, Cal carried a glass half full of Jack Daniels over to the kitchen table and sat down across from Daniel Briggs and Don Maynor. "Anyone else want one of these?" Cal asked, raising his glass.

Daniel shook his head.

"I'll take one," said Maynor.

Cal pointed his thumb back over his shoulder. "Help yourself. Mi casa es su casa."

"You okay?" Daniel asked, concern etched in his expression, as their newest addition headed to the bar.

"I'll be fine. Bad headache. Nothing one of these and some Vitamin M can't handle." Vitamin M was the term Marines affectionately use for Motrin.

"Have you talked to Neil yet?" asked Daniel.

"He texted me a minute ago. Nothing yet. Any ideas?"

"No."

"I'm sure the feds will take care of it." Just then, Cal's phone buzzed with an incoming text. "It's Senator Zimmer. He said I need to turn on a television."

Maynor, finishing his copious whiskey pour, reached over and turned on the oversized television mounted to the wall next to the bar. A moment later, it flickered to life. It was already on the FoxNews Channel.

A message scrolled across the bottom marquis as the news anchor babbled on about the recent attack, images of the scene flashing behind him.

- President to address the nation in two minutes. -

Cal turned his chair to face the television, hoping the address wouldn't add another bale of hay to the search for the elusive needle. The fact that Neil and his team also hadn't found any crumbs in the investigation for the Air and Space attack made Cal nervous. Whoever was coordinating the attacks knew what they were doing. They also knew how to act completely off the grid. Worse still, they probably had help from inside the U.S. government.

+ + +

The president sat in the Oval office, face creased with intensity. More surprisingly, the First Lady stood behind him, mirroring her husband's stern expression.

"Good afternoon, fellow Americans. As most of you know, earlier this morning, at a private concert in the quiet town of Orange Beach, Alabama, an explosion aimed at killing the first lady killed and wounded over two hundred civilians along with singing great Horace Moon. This attack, along with the vice president's murder, is an act of war. I have instructed the directors of the FBI and NSA to pursue all leads. The guilty parties will be found and brought to justice."

His face softened. "I would be remiss if I didn't thank all those who have sent their well wishes to the first lady, and the families of the vice president and the federal agents lost in both attacks. Thank you. Your thoughts and prayers are not in vain.

"For one piece of good news, today I have officially appointed a new vice president to serve out the remaining three years of my term. I am proud to have a strong voice of reason on my side. He is a new friend, but a close one. Over the past year he's become a welcome voice of reason in the nation's capital. Just before going on air, under the auspices of the Chief Justice of the Supreme Court, and with full support of a bi-partisan coalition from the Senate and House, Senator Brandon Zimmer was sworn in as the vice president of the United State of America."

✦ ✦ ✦

"Holy shit," muttered Cal, as the president signed off with, "God Bless America."

"Did you know about this?" asked Daniel.

Cal shook his head. "Brandon didn't say anything."

"Wait," said Maynor. "Do you guys know that Zimmer guy?"

"He's a friend," offered Daniel.

"You're kidding, right?" laughed Maynor.

Cal spun up and out of his chair, sending it crashing to the floor. His cold eyes flashed at the elder Marine, who put his hand up in apology. "Whoa. I didn't mean piss you off, kid."

Daniel watched the scene calmly and said, "Like I said, he's a good friend."

Maynor nodded. "I'm sorry, Cal. Sometimes my mouth runs away."

Cal's body vibrated, like a coiled snake ready to strike. Three cleansing breaths later, he willed himself to calm. "It's okay. I would've said the same thing a couple years ago. You and I might have more in common than I thought, big mouths and all. But don't call me kid."

"Sure thing. Just don't call me gramps."

The two men smiled, the argument resolved.

+ + +

"Who dropped this off?" growled Congressman Peter Quailen.

"It was a messenger, sir. No return address," the hispanic housekeeper said, cowering slightly.

Quailen grunted and looked down at the package, wrapped in brown paper, simple block lettering with *Rep. P. Quailen* on the front. Quailen had let concerns of his own safety wain over the years. Cockiness replaced caution. His recent scandal put him more on edge. He'd made a lot enemies over the years. Any one of them could use the present situation as an excuse to have him killed.

"Juanita, bring a knife and open this package for me."

The housekeeper did as told, sliding a red folder out of the wrapping.

"Open it," ordered Quailen.

She did. Nothing happened. Quailen moved closer to inspect the contents. There was a note stuck to the inside of the folder. Quailen read it....and smiled.

+ + +

Congressman Joel Erling stared at the wall, the same way he had for the past three hours. Two empty vodka bottles, along with the remnants of the last stash of medical grade marijuana, lay nearby. His home phone had been ringing off the hook. He'd had to ask his brother, a petty crook with nowhere else to go, to answer the phones and keep people away from the house.

There'd been the televised video, the subsequent arrest and questioning, protesters at his massive front gate, and two attempted robberies. The cops had taken care of one. His brother had shot the other. Sometimes having a brother with criminal experience came in handy.

Erling didn't know what to do. It was antsy idle time. Too much to think about. Depression. Regret. Anger. Suicide.

A banging at the office door shook him from his gloom. "Go away!"

"Joel, there's someone on the phone for you."

"I said I don't want to talk to anyone unless it's my lawyer."

"The guy says he's got your ticket out. Sounds legit. I think you should talk to him."

Erling stood, wobbling. He tried to shake away the fog. He wanted to believe. "I'll take it in here."

"He's on line three," came the muffled voice from behind the door.

Erling took a deep breath, and looked up at the ceiling. It was the closest he'd come to saying a prayer in years. "Hello?" said Erling into the phone.

"Joel, it's Pete Quailen. We need to talk."

Chapter 16
United States Naval Observatory, U.S.
Vice President's Residence
9:30pm, December 18th

"**WHY DIDN'T** you tell me?" asked Cal.

Vice President Brandon Zimmer exhaled. "He asked me right after he saw you at the airport. Came straight to my office."

"I can't believe you said yes."

Zimmer's eyes flashed. "What else should I have done? He said he needed my help."

Cal shook his head. "I don't know. Sounds like you really stepped in this time, Mister Vice President."

Zimmer settled. "Tell me about it."

"I know you're busy, but I wanted to ask you about the attacks. What are your thoughts?"

"I don't know. Other than killing my predecessor and trying to kill the first lady, I'm having a hard time coming up with a possible motive," said Zimmer. "Have you found anything?"

"Zip. Neil's got our full resources behind it. Nothing so far."

Both men sat silent for a moment, each lost in their own thoughts. Cal broke the spell. "What's it like being the vice president and not being married?"

Zimmer grinned. "Ask me again in a couple weeks."

"Any plans yet? Do they have you traveling the world on parade?"

"Not yet. I told the president I wanted to get settled. Besides, I have no idea what's going on inside the administration. It'll take time to learn the personalities and the inner workings."

"Sounds like the time they made me a squad leader as a Lance Corporal, except, of course, that you're the new vice president of United States and I was making sure my Marines didn't get in fights at the Driftwood."

"What's the Driftwood?" asked Zimmer.

Cal laughed. "It's a strip club outside Camp Lejeune. Really classy. Remind me to take you there sometime."

"Thanks. I think I'll pass." The vice president's face turned serious. "On another note, the president wants me to oversee the operation..."

"Operation Pest Control," offered Cal.

"That's what you called it?"

Cal shrugged. "Seemed fitting."

Zimmer shook his head, still getting used to the Marine's sense of humor. "Anyway, the president wanted me to support you in any way I can. I'm not sure I'll be of much help yet, but at least he won't have to be directly involved. I'll update him as needed."

That sounded good to Cal. It wasn't that he didn't like the president, but dealing with Zimmer would be easier. They'd forged their friendship against common enemies, and understood each other's strengths. "Okay. The biggest thing you can do for us is make sure the word doesn't get out. Washington is full of leaks, and if word of what we're doing gets around..."

The thought hung in the air, a warning for both men to tread carefully.

"Tell me what your next move is and I'll figure out a way to help."

✛ ✛ ✛

"Like I said, I want this all over the news. I've got my people contacting friends up there. You just do your job and the media will think you're a hero."

"You sure the feds are gonna support this?"

"After they see what I've got, hell yes."

"I don't want to look like an idiot. You'll tell me if anything changes?"

"Of course. Hey, did you pick a week to stay at my place in Key West? It'll be open all February."

"Yeah. The second week would be perfect. Thanks for that."

"No problem. Any time."

Congressman Peter Quailen clicked off the call and smiled. Things were falling into place.

✛ ✛ ✛

Agent Steve Stricklin sat nursing his splitting headache with a frozen daiquiri. He wasn't much for hard alcohol, but needed something to soothe the pain before the meds kicked in.

Earlier, he'd gotten a royal ass-chewing from his boss, who'd found out that Stricklin had not been at the bombing site when the explosion occurred.

Thank God, Stricklin had thought, as his boss railed on about having an FBI presence available. Stricklin explained how he'd left to follow a lead and narrowly missed becoming one of the bombing victims. "I was right next to where the guy was standing," Stricklin lied. He'd been farther away than Cal.

It was a new politically correct FBI, and Stricklin's boss relented. "Fine. Just make sure you're around to help out if you're needed."

Stricklin pressed the oversized margarita glass against his forehead. The pieces were coming back. The only explanation of how he'd ended up on the ground was that one of the Marines had sucker punched him. Ideas flitted into his stream of conscious. A plan formed as he swirled the slush in his glass and stared at the young bartender with the cut-off jeans. Stokes and his friends would pay.

Chapter 17
Camp Spartan, Arrington, TN
5:52am, December 19th

THE OLD SCHOOL weight room was half full. Travis Haden dripped with sweat, straining to push out his last set of squats. MSgt Willy Trent stood behind him, ready to assist.

"You've got this," said Trent.

Travis, sweat glistening on his forehead, gritted his teeth and pushed until the bar jumped up and over the holders. He backed out of the frame. "Jeez. Used to be a lot easier."

Trent laughed, "We're not as young as we used to be."

"I don't see you losing many steps, Top."

It was true. MSgt Trent was one of those freaks of nature. Despite his age, he only seemed to get stronger and faster. This frustrated the SEAL to no end. Although Travis could outrun, outlift and outfight 99.99% of the men in the world, the competitor in him always looked at the huge Marine with a hint of jealousy.

"Maybe you should've been a Marine instead, Trav. I think it's the uniform and the ladies. Keeps us young."

Travis grinned. "I can't argue with that."

They showered in the locker room, then headed to the chow hall for breakfast. The CEO of SSI liked to eat at least one meal a day with his troops. Besides, it was pancake day, and Travis deserved it. If you could survive a workout with Trent, anyone deserved a hearty meal.

The mismatched pair said their hellos as they walked into the dining facility. Most were greeted by name. Trent moved to do a walk-through of the back of the chow line. As SSI's unofficial head of food services, Trent spent many hours helping out in the kitchen, keeping his culinary skills sharp.

Travis moved along the empty line quickly, and then took a seat. Before he could take his first bite, his cell phone rang.

"This better be good. I was about to take a bite of a strawberry pancake."

"Sir, it's Isen from the main gate."

"What's up?"

"Sir, there's a large group of police and reporters wanting to see you. They wouldn't show me a warrant or anything. What you want me to do?"

Alarm bells went off in Travis's head, but by looking at him you wouldn't know it. "Have Ms. Haines and Mr. Dunn meet me at the front gate. I'll be there in a couple minutes."

Travis rose and headed to the line to find Trent, who was tasting the gravy and explaining to a new hire that perhaps more flour should be added to the roux. He looked up when Travis approached.

"I need you to come with me, Top."

Trent patted the young chef on the back and followed Travis out the side door.

+ + +

Marge "The Hammer" Haines was the first one to the gate, and was peppering a policeman with questions when Travis arrived. "What's going on?" he asked, trying to ignore the flash of reporters' camera bulbs and the glare of lights extended from the tops of television news vans.

"They say they're here to arrest you," Haines fumed.

"For what?"

"He won't say. Supposedly it's a matter of national security."

Travis's eyebrow rose. "And they want *me*?"

Haines nodded. "Let me get on the phone and straighten this out."

Travis shook his head. "It's all right. Why don't I go with Officer..."

"Labeau," offered the slightly overweight plainclothes policeman, who was looking a little too smug.

Haines hesitated, and then turned to face Officer Labeau. "Mr. Haden will ride in one of our vehicles and follow you to the station."

"Those aren't the orders..."

Haines cut him off. "It's either that or I call up the governor, who happens to be a good friend of Mr. Haden, and have him talk to your superiors."

Labeau relented, wisely avoiding the powerful attorney's threat. "Okay. He can have a driver and follow me."

"Top, how about we take your truck?" asked Travis nonchalantly, as if they were going to the grocery store.

"No problem. I'll run and get it."

Minutes later, Travis and Trent pulled out of the SSI compound, soon to be surrounded by a phalanx of red and blue flashing vehicles. Haines was already on the phone.

✛ ✛ ✛

BREAKING NEWS

"The Metropolitan Nashville Police Department has confirmed that the CEO of Stokes Security International, based in Arrington, Tennessee, has been brought in for questioning. Our sources from inside the nation's capital tell us that it may have to do with the terrorist attacks at the National Air and Space Museum and in Orange Beach, Alabama yesterday. White House officials have not yet responded to our requests for a statement."

✚ ✚ ✚

"What the hell happened?" Cal asked Todd Dunn, director of internal security at SSI, over the phone.

"Haines is on it, Cal. The skipper's been with the Nashville PD for just under an hour. He can take care of himself."

"I'm not worried about Travis. He's a big boy. What about SSI? What's the possible fallout?"

"Your guess is as good as mine. As long as we get this cleared up fast, I think we'll be okay. If we don't…"

"Then we're screwed," finished Cal. He ran through his options. Since getting out of the Marine Corps, Cal had avoided the politics of running his father's company. Of course, it was *his* company, and he didn't want to see its name dragged through the mud by a ridiculous claim. "Who's running the investigation? I can't believe the feds are letting the locals do it."

"I think they'll be swooping in at any moment. They're probably trying to get more information before deploying assets. Besides, Haines already made the calls to our high-level contacts at the major agencies. They know that if they lift a finger in the wrong direction, she'll be all over them."

Cal said a silent thanks to his deceased father for having the foresight to hire the skilled attorney. Her reputation alone could keep the wolves at bay until they could find the culprit.

"Let's stay in touch."

"You got it."

+ + +

"Bueno?" answered Gaucho, who sat watching the news with the rest of his team, stroking his braided beard, deep in thought. They'd all been shocked to see their CEO, who also happened to be a good friend, taken into custody.

"It's Cal."

"Hey, boss. We were just watching the news. Sorry about Travis."

"Yeah. Thanks. Look, me and Briggs are in Arlington. How quickly can you and your boys get up here from Charlottesville?"

"In civvies?"

"Yeah, with concealed."

"Driving fast, probably two hours. In the helo, under an hour."

"We may need the vehicles, so why don't you drive. Leave as soon as you can."

"You got it, boss."

Gaucho stood up and turned off the television.

"Saddle up, homies."

+ + +

"They're on their way," announced Cal.

Daniel nodded and Don Maynor asked, "Who?"

"The cavalry. I've gotta go see the president." He pointed at Daniel. "You come with me. Maynor, you want us to get you a flight home?"

"Nah. I think I'll stick around. Haven't been up here in ages. Want to go pay my respects to the Iwo Jima Memorial. Hell, you might need me again."

"Use the house for as long as you need. Daniel will give you the code. If you decide to leave, send us the receipt for your flight home."

+ + +

As the two Marines slid into the rental vehicle, Daniel turned to his boss. "What are we going to see the president about?"

Scowling, Cal said, "To find the leak."

Chapter 18
The White House, District of Columbia
8:26am, December 19th

"**THANK YOU** for seeing us on such short notice, Mr. President," said Cal, his demeanor neutral, tone clipped.

The president looked up from the folder stamped *Top Secret Presidential*. "You said it was urgent. Should we wait for the vice president? He's on his way."

It took Cal a moment to remember that the vice president was his friend, former Senator Brandon Zimmer. "That might be a good idea, sir."

"Why don't you and Briggs have a seat. I'll have them bring in some water and snacks while we're waiting. I haven't eaten today."

Cal didn't argue, instead sitting down on the love seat across from Daniel, who gave him a look as if to say, "Calm down."

No one said a word until Vice President Zimmer entered. Daniel immediately moved to stand. Cal motioned for him to stay seated. Zimmer either didn't notice or didn't care, instead taking the seat next to Daniel. He looked tired, and it was barely his second day on the job.

"What's on your mind, Cal? I take it by your demeanor that this isn't a social call?" asked the president, as he joined the others.

Inside, Cal simmered. He willed his temper down. "Mr. President, I assume you've heard about my cousin, the CEO of SSI, Travis Haden, being arrested this morning?"

"I thought he was taken in for questioning," answered the President.

Cal's jaw clenched. "Sir, they showed up at our Nashville headquarters with a caravan of ten police cars and an entourage of reporters."

The president's eyes narrowed. "I didn't hear about that."

"What are you thinking, Cal?" asked Zimmer.

"First, you both know there's no way in hell we were involved in the attacks targeting the first lady..."

"We would never say—," interrupted the President. Cal dared to raise his hand to quiet the most powerful man in the world.

"I'm not finished, Mr. President. When I agreed to undertake this operation, it was with the understanding that the only people privy to the full thing were the men in this room. We kept our end of the bargain, sir."

The accusation stabbed.

"And you're saying we didn't," responded the president.

Cal nodded.

The President exhaled. "We haven't told anyone, son. Not even my closest staff—."

"And yet my company's name is now being tarnished by the liberal nuts on television, saying that we're part of some right-wing conspiracy. More than one client is demanding answers. I warn you, Mr. President, if you can't find out who did this, I will."

"That's enough, Cal," barked Zimmer. Cal glared at his friend, but kept his mouth shut after the rebuke. Silence. Then Zimmer asked, "Why do you think the leak is from here? Besides, why would anyone want to link you to the attacks? There's no evidence to support the claim. Trav will be home before noon."

"With all due respect, *sir*, that's not the point. Of course we're innocent. But the threat is still out there. We've been accused. You, Mr. President, should know more than the rest of us what a media frenzy can do to a company's reputation. Besides, who the hell would have the pull to get the Nashville police *and* the media to show up at the same time and the same place?" Cal asked. When no one answered, he continued. "I'll tell you who it is. The only demographic that has that kind of pull, that can be that Machiavellian, are politicians. When I think politics, my gaze rests right here, on Washington, D.C."

+ + +

"What do you mean you can't throw him in jail? And what the fuck happened to all the video? It was supposed to look like you guys were taking down a drug kingpin."

"They got some big shot lawyer that made some calls. She shut down most of the news channels with threats of lawsuits."

"You're saying some *bitch* had the balls to get in my way?"

"Look, I'm doing what I can, but I already got my ass handed to me from the chief. He's pissed that I took that many guys with me. He said I was showboating."

"I don't give a flying fuck what that fat shit says! Don't ever forget that you work for me, and that you've worked for me since your pimply ass left the academy. Now get off the phone and do what you're being paid to do!"

Congressman Peter Quailen smiled wide. His tirade had been more of an act to keep that shit Lebeau in his place. The media coverage hadn't been what he'd planned, but that wasn't a problem. The damage had been done. Quailen dialed another number and said, "Is my money in the account?"

+ + +

Cal was still fuming as he rushed to leave the White House. Daniel stayed close behind, worried that they'd just stepped over the line. The meeting hadn't ended well. Cal, in not so many words, had told the president that he had enough secrets to make his last three years in the White House very miserable. The president hadn't taken it well, telling Cal to take some time to cool off. Zimmer had tried to pull Cal aside on the way out, but the stubborn Marine brushed by, making a B-line for the exit.

Minutes later they got in the car, and Cal slammed his palm on the dashboard. "Fuck!"

"You okay?" asked Daniel, knowing the temper that rarely surfaced from the young leader.

Cal stared out the rain streaked window, not saying a thing until they'd pulled onto the Beltway.

"What do you think? You think the president ran his mouth?" asked Cal.

Daniel shrugged. "Above my pay grade, boss."

Cal rolled his eyes. "Seriously. Who do you think did this?"

"I don't know. How many people have you pissed off in the last three years?"

Cal laughed. "Are you kidding me? With all the scumbags we've put away or killed, the list is long."

"Do you really think it was someone on the president's staff? That would be pretty ballsy doing that under his nose."

"I don't put anything past politicians. If there's one thing I've learned, it's that they'll say or do anything to get their way."

"They're not all bad. What about Brandon?"

Cal snorted. "He's no Boy Scout either. Don't ever forget how we all met."

+ + +

"What do we need to do about Stokes?" asked the president.

"Let's give him a day to cool off, and then I'll talk to him," said Zimmer. "I'd be pissed too. I'm just sorry he came in here like that. If I had known..."

"It's not your fault. I can't say that I blame him. There was a time when I would've done the same thing." The president walked over to the fireplace, staring into the flames. "Cal's right about one thing. We need to help him find whoever's behind this."

Chapter 19
SSI Safe House, Arlington, VA
10:19am, December 19th

THE FOUR VEHICLES pulled into the drive, Gaucho and his team piling out. They quickly unloaded two duffel bags per man and went inside.

"Any trouble getting here?" asked Cal, as Gaucho stepped into the dining room.

"We left in intervals and met halfway, caravanned the rest. Had a tail. Think it was a reporter. Lost her pretty quick."

"You sure?"

Gaucho rolled his eyes. "Any word on the skipper and Trent? They get out yet?"

"Not yet. Haines is working on it."

"I heard she went apeshit. I know I'm a crazy Mexican, but ain't no way I'd ever piss off The Hammer."

"Yeah," said Cal absently.

Gaucho glanced at Daniel. "What did we miss?"

Daniel pointed to Cal, who looked up from his thoughts. "We paid a visit to the president earlier."

"Yeah? How'd it go? They know who's behind the attacks?"

"Not yet."

"So what's the plan? Got somewhere for us to go?" asked Gaucho.

"Get the boys together and I'll go over what we know so far. We're on standby until we hear from either Zimmer or Neil."

Gaucho nodded, and left to coordinate the dispersal of gear, worried about his boss's attitude. He hadn't seen Cal this detached before, except for when they'd lost men in Jackson Hole. Not a man to be afraid of much, Cal's lack of typical optimism worried the former Delta operator.

✚ ✚ ✚

"Come on, guys. We've gotta have something by now," Neil complained to his team of computer geeks. "Nothing from the NSA?"

"Nada," answered a guy with a head full of curly red hair, sporting white rimmed oversized glasses without lenses.

Neil was at a loss. He thought for sure they'd have something. His automated programs scoured the world, trying to find any link to Travis's arrest, while also monitoring activity for information on the terrorist attacks. Still nothing. Whoever was behind the operation knew what they were doing. To Neil's highly tuned mind, it wasn't the acts that necessarily bothered him, it was the subsequent silence.

✦ ✦ ✦

Special Agent Stricklin spent the previous night helping at The Amphitheatre at the Wharf, keeping reporters and nosy locals at bay, meanwhile freezing his ass off, still nursing a wicked headache.

He'd gotten out of going back the following morning by telling the agent in charge that he had to go to the hospital to get his head checked out. The agent in charge didn't argue, despite needing the manpower. Stricklin had already pissed off half his staff, and he was glad to be rid of the guy.

Stricklin sat in his hotel, engrossed in reading every article he could find on the arrest of SSI's CEO. His heart leapt when an article by The Tennessean referenced the majority owner of Stokes Security International, Calvin Stokes, Jr.

The pieces started coming together in Stricklin's head. If he could only connect Stokes to the amphitheater attack and an assault on a federal officer...

Clicking a new tab, Stricklin started a new search. He had to get to D.C.

+ + +

"Mr. President, I think we may have something," announced the president's chief of staff, walking into the Oval Office.

The President looked up from his work. "What's that?"

"We may have a lead on the Orange Beach attacker." Vance handed over a thin folder.

The President scanned its contents. "Give me a minute, Rick. I need to make a call."

Once his chief of staff had closed the door, the president picked up his desk phone. "Connect me to Cal Stokes."

+ + +

"Yes, sir. Thank you, Mr. President." Cal glanced up after ending the call. He'd stepped out on the porch for privacy, and walked back in the living room, motioning for Gaucho and Daniel to follow him to the kitchen.

"What's up?" asked Gaucho, now seated on a bar stool as Cal poured himself a glass of water.

"The president says they just found out from the Alabama bomber's family that the guy was up in Detroit for the last two weeks doing some training with a new trucking company. They said he'd been acting strange ever since coming home."

"What are the Secret Service doing about it?" asked Daniel.

"They were able to track the location from the guy's cell phone trail. The FBI's going in to raid the place. He said he'll have Zimmer call us when they know more."

"I went to Detroit once with my abuelito," said Gaucho. "Good coney dogs, but cold as shit."

+ + +

The FBI SWAT team crept silently through the maze of abandoned buildings. Detroit was full of them. A barren wasteland. The address they'd been given showed a long-vacant auto manufacturing factory. It'd seen better days, crumbling and covered in graffiti, choked with debris.

"Two minutes," the point man whispered into his mic, never slowing his approach.

His weapon swiveled as a homeless man sitting next to a small fire startled, jingling the bag of aluminum cans lying next to him. The second man in line put his finger to his lips, instantly hushing any forthcoming sound from the bum. Someone farther back in line would take him in for questioning.

"Thirty seconds," announced the lead agent, each subsequent team member steeling themselves for entry. They spread out, covering every approach as well as they could. The place was an ambusher's dream. Angles and vantage points mocked the team's advance, goading them forward.

The point man was the first in, scanning, pivoting, swiveling. Nothing. Room to room they went. Still nothing.

Closing in on the central fabrication area, the point man halted their assault, and then touched his nose and pointed forward. There was a smell of roasted meat coming from up ahead. Not meat, but some kind of flesh. The man leading the move had done a stint in Iraq training with Marine Special Forces. He'd encountered scenes that still brought back vivid memories. For him, more than anything, it was the smell, the same stench he sensed creeping forward now.

Coming around a corner, he finally spotted the source of the fire. Eyes widening in disgust, he waved his squad forward.

Chapter 20
SSI Safe House, Arlington, VA
12:41pm, December 19th

"IS THIS for real?" said one of the SSI operators over Cal's shoulder. They were all viewing the oversized computer screen.

"Yeah. The FBI just sent it over. The president's probably watching it right now, too," answered Cal.

"Whoever did this is a bunch of sick fuckers, boss," growled Gaucho, the hair on the back of his neck matching the sentiment in the room.

The team watched as the video panned around the factory room. Rusted racks lined the room under old rail systems that used to move vehicles from one portion of the factory to another. From one of those racks hung five burning bodies, just then being doused by SWAT members.

"I'll bet that reeks," said another one the SSI crew. They were all experienced men, from all branches of the armed services. They'd seen and smelled the aftereffects of acts like the one being shown on the computer screen.

The room hushed as the camera zoomed in on a gurney, dirty surgical equipment arrayed on a metal tray, covered in blood.

"I saw a bomb factory in Iraq a couple years ago," said Cal. "Looked a lot like that. They were putting IEDs inside little kids. If they didn't die, they kept them there for a day, then sent them out to sell DVDs to our Marines."

More than one man nodded, having experienced something similar during their time overseas. The cameraman did a thorough job capturing every inch of the surgical area, and then moved to the left, focusing on the back wall. Cal paused the playback. "Oh, shit."

+ + +

The president paced, taking pulls from a cigarette stolen from his hidden stash. He'd tried to quit for years, trying everything from the patch to pills and electronic cigarettes. At times the stress pulled out his old habit. It was the video and its message.

Vice President Zimmer, the chief of staff and the president's National Security Adviser were in opposite corners, talking into their cell phones, trying to do what they could to deal with the situation.

The image replayed over and over again in his mind's eye. Aryan propaganda. Death to the Jews. Death to the Hispanics. Death to blacks. And then...a caricatured spray painting of the first lady, adorned with a bullseye on her forehead.

✦ ✦ ✦

"How's the president doing?"

"Not good, Cal," answered Zimmer, glancing over his shoulder at the still-pacing head of state. "Seeing the first lady's face on the video really shook him up. Rick Vance says he's never seen him like this."

"Is there anything we can do?" asked Cal, genuinely concerned for the president, despite their run-in earlier. Cal had lost the love of his life. He knew the pain of it, and could imagine what the chief executive was thinking.

"You still in Arlington?"

"Yeah."

"Good. Stay close. The way the president's talking, whenever we find out who's behind this, it'll be taken care of outside of official channels. That means you."

Cal couldn't believe what he was hearing. Outing dirty politicians was one thing. It was hands-off. Going in and taking care of terrorists on U.S. soil was something else entirely.

"Not that I'm complaining, but are you sure that's a good idea? Wouldn't one of the agencies be better suited to taking care of it? I don't want anyone changing their mind halfway in," said Cal.

"This just got personal, Cal. I know you understand that. Let's just call it a shift in presidential policy."

"Fair enough. Tell the president that we'll be ready whenever he calls."

+ + +

"Did you get the bodies burned?"

"Yeah. We almost didn't make it out in time."

"How many do you have left?"

"Three."

"All viable?"

"As viable as they can be."

"Good. I'll be in touch soon."

Chapter 21
Litchfield Golf Course, Litchfield, Minnesota
3:25pm, December 19th

THE FRIGID AIR whipped off of Lake Ripley, causing swirls of snow dust to sweep across the closed golf course. In the distance, a large engine revved, working against the brutal Minnesota snow and ice. A minute later a Ford F450 rolled into the shuttered clubhouse parking lot.

The driver stepped out in the subzero air, face obscured for protection from the elements rather than anonymity. He wasn't worried about being recognized. No one else was crazy enough to be out in the cold. A light flashed from the opposite end of the building, and he headed that way.

Sheltered from the wind, another man, daring to smoke a cigarette, waited. The newcomer approached nonchalantly. They'd had similar meetings around town for the past year. Money always changed hands. Good paydays for the Minnesota native.

The driver of the large Ford pulled a sealed freezer bag out of his coat. "This is the last batch. The rest got shipped overseas."

"That's okay. This'll be the last one we need."

The Minnesotan was disappointed. He'd known the relationship with the strange man would end at some point, but the money was good, good enough to buy himself the truck he'd arrived in along with a couple vacations for him and the wife.

"You have the money?"

The smoking man pointed to a plain black backpack on the ground, the same kind he'd delivered every time before.

"Mind if I take a look?" asked the Minnesotan.

The smoker shrugged, unconcerned. After examining the contents of the bag, the supplier stood back up. "Looks good. Here's your stuff."

Taking the sealed baggie without examining it, the buyer asked, "I assume it's the same as the others?"

"Of course."

"Good." He stuffed the purchase into his fur-lined jacket with his left hand. His right hand stubbed and discarded the cigarette, and entered the opposite pocket. A split second later, it came out again holding a silenced .22 pistol, that promptly spat two rounds into the supplier's face. The lifeless body crumpled to the ground.

Grabbing one of the smaller stacks of cash, along with two tiny dime bags from his pants pocket, the buyer stuck them in the man's oversized hand, tucking it under the body slightly.

After snatching the backpack of cash, he walked calmly to a rental SUV idling on the other side of the road. He had to get to FedEx before they closed.

✛ ✛ ✛

Springfield, VA
4:45pm

"Stevie, what are you doing home so early? You told me you'd be gone two more weeks!" screeched Mrs. Stricklin, hugging her son as he stepped in from the cold.

"Change of plans, Ma. Have any food made?" Special Agent Stricklin tossed his overnight bag on the kitchen table and grabbed a beer from the fridge.

"Not right now, but I can make you something."

Stricklin nodded and headed downstairs to his bedroom. It was a split level, and for the most part, his mother left him alone when he was in town. It was expensive living in D.C., so he'd opted to stay in a suburb with his widowed mother. She liked having him close. He liked not having to pay rent.

After two more beers from the fridge in his room — his mother kept it stocked — Stricklin headed back to the kitchen, following the smell of shrimp and stew. Without a word, he grabbed a hunk of bread, a bowl, and ladled a bowl full of the gently simmering concoction.

As usual, it was delicious. Mrs. Stricklin, rail thin, sat across from her only son. "How long will you be home, Stevie?"

"Come on, Ma, can't you call me Steve?"

"Sorry. I know. It's just that you'll always be my little Stevie." A wistful look followed. There had been many of those looks after his father's death years before. "So how's work, mister big shot FBI agent?"

Stricklin shrugged. "Not bad. I was at the terrorist attack in Alabama."

His mother inhaled sharply. "Did you get hurt? The news said there were a lot of people killed."

Stricklin pointed to the bruise on the side of his head. "Just a bruise. I'm okay."

"Did you go to the doctor? Do you have a concussion? Can you hear okay?"

He nodded as he continued eating, enjoying the attention. "I'm fine."

"It's like I told you before you went in the Marines, you've got to take care of yourself, son. You're all I've got left."

Stricklin hated it when she got all weepy. Sometimes he wondered if it wouldn't have been easier if she died with her husband in the car wreck.

"Your uncle called. Did I tell you?" she asked.

"What did he want?"

"He phoned last night and said he was coming in town."

"Today?"

"Yes. He said he wanted you to call him. I thought I'd sent you a text like you showed me, but, well, you know I mess that up sometimes."

Stricklin simmered. It would've been good to have that information the night before. "I'll call him after I finish eating."

"Good. I know he'd love to see you. He's always asking about what you're doing."

+ + +

Stricklin, dressed in his best suit, following the directions on his GPS, finally came to an ornately sculpted iron gate tucked back in a pricey Falls Church neighborhood. The gate squealed open. He pulled through, following the short curving drive up to the mansion.

His uncle, probably half in the bag, greeted him at the front door. "Stevie! Look at you. You look good, kid!"

Stricklin smiled. "Thanks, Uncle Pete. I appreciate you having me over. Your new place is beautiful."

Congressman Peter Quailen looked up at his house, as if he was just realizing it was there. "Yeah, it's not bad, right?"

Chapter 22
SSI Safe House, Arlington, VA
7:28pm, December 19th

DON MAYNOR parked his rented Harley, taking in the newly arrived vehicles. Grabbing his bike bag, he walked to the front door and knocked. Gaucho answered the door. "Can I help you?"

"Yeah, I'm here with Cal Stokes. I'm—."

"Oh. You're the other jarhead."

Maynor grinned. "Don Maynor." The two men shook. "Let me guess. Army?"

"Guilty, hombre. Name's Gaucho. Come on in."

Maynor followed the short Latino into the house, which now looked more like a staging area. There were weapons stacked neatly inside the dining area where

Cal sat conferring with Daniel. The Marines looked up from their conversation.

"Look what the cat dragged in," said Cal. "Have fun on libbo, Lance Corporal?"

Maynor chuckled. "Yeah. Got to see some old buddies. They even let me in Eight and I looking like this."

"You should've told me you were heading over there. My old platoon commander is with the Silent Drill Platoon. I'm sure he would've given you the royal tour."

"No problem. A nice female Corporal gave me a tour in exchange for a cruise around town on my bike."

"Sounds like I need to take dating lessons from you," joked Gaucho.

"What can I say? I may be old, but I'm still a Marine. More than I can say for you and your *Army of One*." Maynor spent a good deal of time with old vets in Orange Beach, but it'd been a while since he'd talked to the boys still holding down the fort. The old warrior felt the irresistible pull to be part of it.

Gaucho shook his head and clapped the senior Marine on the back. "You'll sure as shit fit in around here, gramps."

Maynor gave him a middle finger, but smiled back.

"Enough grab-assing, Marine," said Cal, enjoying the back and forth. "Time to get to work."

Maynor took a seat at the table. "What did I miss?"

"First things first. I know I don't need to say this, but I will. What I'm about to tell you is Top Secret Presidential. That means that if you run off at the mouth, you will either spend the rest of your life in a ten by ten cell, or be shot in the back of the head."

"Got it."

"Okay. Here's what we found."

+ + +

Stricklin was halfway into his fourth glass of bourbon when they made their way to his uncle's parlor. Quailen called it his smoking room.

"I had a special air filtration system installed. Lets me smoke all the cigars I want and not get it in the rest of the house."

Stricklin took it all in. Coming from a modest background, the rare visits with his uncle never ceased to bring out a craving. He still remembered his first visit to New Orleans. It was in seventh grade. Quailen was an up-and-coming congressman, full of energy, enjoying the adoration of his constituency. He'd been a gracious host, taking young Steve on a deep sea fishing charter, giving him his first Hurricane on Bourbon Street, even getting him a blow job at a swanky massage parlor. "After this weekend, you're officially a man," his uncle had proclaimed.

He knew about the video of Quailen that was making the rounds on YouTube, racking up millions of views, but didn't bring it up. Better to keep things cordial and enjoy the opulence that he'd always wanted.

Congressman Quailen pulled out two thick cigars, clipping both expertly and handing one to Stricklin. "Got these from a guy down in Cuba. They say he's the best roller around."

They sat, enjoying the musty bitterness, staring into the blazing fire. Stricklin downed the rest of his glass, nestling back comfortably into the leather armchair.

"How's work? They keeping you busy?" asked Quailen.

Stricklin shrugged. "It's okay. You hear that I was down in Alabama when the bomb went off yesterday?"

Quailen feigned surprise. He'd already done his homework. "You were? Was it as bad as they say?"

Stricklin grimaced. "It was pretty bad, Uncle Pete. Body parts everywhere."

"They any closer to finding the people behind it?"

Hesitating, Stricklin searched for the right words. He wanted to impress his uncle. Despite the scandal, the media was already saying the wily congressman would probably come out relatively unscathed. The familial relationship could come in handy. "The Secret Service are a bunch of idiots. Most of those meatheads probably dropped out of the FBI Academy." Stricklin stood up, somewhat shakily, and walked over to pour himself another drink. Quailen watched expectantly. "I've got my own idea, though, if only someone would listen."

"Why don't you tell me? Maybe I can help."

"I don't know, Uncle Pete. It's still an ongoing investigation."

"That's okay. I know you're a by-the-book kinda guy. I don't want you to get in trouble," said Quailen, apologetically. "Tell you what. I may have some information that could help."

Stricklin turned around cautiously. *I've got him*, thought Quailen.

"What do you have?" asked Stricklin.

"No. Don't worry about it. You're right. The last thing I want is to get your ass in a crack. Forget I said anything."

"That's okay. How about I take a look? Hell, I'm an FBI agent. I know how to keep my mouth shut."

Quailen sat pondering, but not really. He'd played his nephew perfectly. The poor kid would never have the guts to be a real leader, but that didn't mean he couldn't have his uses. Finally, Quailen acquiesced. "Okay. But don't tell anyone where you got this."

He stood up and walked to the wall of books, complete with a tracked ladder to reach the highest shelves. Pausing, as if remembering where he'd put it, Quailen slowly pulled out a large, and most likely priceless, tome. From inside he extracted a manilla envelope.

"Like I said, I'm not sure this will help, but I hope it does." Quailen handed the parcel to Stricklin, who opened it with slightly shaking hands, extracting the papers within.

His eyes widened as he scanned the contents. *This is my ticket.*

+ + +

"Anyone have any questions?" asked Cal, after finishing the latest briefing. There hadn't been any updates from Neil or Zimmer. They were still flying blind, standing by.

"What about the bodies from Detroit? Any IDs?" Daniel questioned.

"Zimmer said the FBI's on it, but that it could take a while."

"What about the homeless guy? Did they get anything from him?" asked Gaucho.

"They said the guy was high as a kite. Could barely say his own name. Dead end."

The day felt like a waste to Cal. Instead of doing something, they'd waited for updates from the vice president. Cal wasn't good at waiting. He wanted to be doing anything but just sitting around.

"Hey, you said earlier that the kid who blew himself up in Alabama..." started Maynor.

"Lincoln," offered Daniel.

"Right. Michael Lincoln. You said his parents thought he was up in Detroit for training."

"Yeah?"

"Well, I'm friends with some guys who are retired, but do the occasional hauling. They like the cash. Anyway, one of the guys, Lenny, he's kind of a racist prick, but I don't mind taking his money playing poker. Well, he mentioned something about an invite he got to go up to the Motor City. He said there was good money in it. Some kind of training for the fracking they're doing in the Dakotas. Big business," explained Maynor.

"Did he go?" asked Cal, hoping.

"No. He got hurt the week before."

"What about the other truckers?"

"Nah. I asked and they said they didn't get an invite. They told me that one of the companies Lenny hauls for is owned by a member of some Aryan club. Rumor is they only hire like minded drivers, sometimes adding extra cargo for shipment."

"Might be worth looking into. Do you think you could call your poker buddy and find out about the company?"

"No problem. I'll tell him I'm looking to make some extra dough. He knows I do odds and ends," said Maynor.

"Perfect."

As they dispersed, Cal's phone rang. He looked down. It was someone calling from Camp Spartan.

"Stokes."

"Mr. Stokes, this is the SSI switchboard. I have a Special Agent Stricklin on the line. Would you like for me to patch him through?"

The hair on the back of Cal's neck stood up.

"Go ahead."

The line clicked. Stokes said, "Hello?"

"Stokes, this is Special Agent Stricklin."

"What do you want Stricklin?" spat Cal, tempted to cut the call.

"I don't want anything," came the haughty reply.

"Then why I are you calling me?"

Stricklin laughed. "An interesting piece of evidence just came to my attention, and I just wanted to let you know that I am personally going to take you and your company down."

Chapter 23
SSI Headquarters I, Camp Spartan, Arrington, TN
11:18pm EST, December 19th

"**YEAH?**" answered Neil, stifling a yawn. It'd been a long day at headquarters. Travis and MSgt Trent had returned earlier, both a bit impatient, but none the worse for wear. The trip to the police station was pointless for both sides, as Marge Haines's handiwork prevented the cops from questioning SSI's top man. The best the Nashville PD could do was put the two men — Trent had refused to leave his boss alone — in an interrogation room where they were supplied with a constant flow of coffee and donuts.

"It's Cal. I need you to do something for me."

"What's up?"

"I need you to trace the phone number that just called SSI's main line. How long will that take?"

Neil's mind snapped into place. "Give me five minutes."

Clearing screens in a whir, Neil clicked and typed, accessing highly encrypted telephone databases. To his genius level skills, it was all child's play. Unlike their previous search for a needle in a haystack, he had a focal point.

"Got it." He dialed Cal back.

"What did you find?"

"The call came from Falls Church, not far from you."

"Give me the address."

Neil did.

"Do you know who owns the surrounding properties?" asked Cal.

"Working on that now. The satellites images show a single property, pretty big. It's loading."

Neil scrolled through the tax records, which listed a corporation, Kingstown LLC, as the owner. Cross-referencing government resources, Neil clicked his way deeper into the ownership of Kingstown LLC. His finger stopped over a single name. "Oh crap."

"What is it?"

"You're not gonna like this, Cal."

"Tell me."

+ + +

Quailen had excused himself to make a phone call, leaving his nephew in the lounge.

"Is everything ready?"

"Yes, sir."

"Good. You know where to find me."

✝ ✝ ✝

"Gaucho, get the boys up. We're hitting the road," commanded Cal.

"Where to?" Gaucho was up and ready.

"Just down the road."

Twenty minutes later, the team, scattered in five vehicles throughout the target neighborhood, sat waiting. Each vehicle had one remote drone aloft, reconnoitering the area with infrared video.

"We've got at least ten bogies patrolling the property. Looks like there's at least five more inside," announced Daniel.

Cal sat, watching the small screen as Daniel maneuvered the tiny craft. The vehicles were version 2.0 of Neil's 'Baby Bird' invention. Launched and controlled via a pair of glasses, the little crafts were a mainstay in the SSI arsenal. Silent and versatile, the operators never started an operation without them.

"What are our options?" asked Cal, eager to take action.

"We can sit and wait," said Gaucho. "Maybe your guy will come out."

Cal didn't like the idea of waiting around. It wasn't his style. "I'm going in," he announced.

"No way, boss," said Gaucho. "Too many bad guys."

"I'll go with you," said the ever unflinching Daniel. "You're not going in alone."

"Fine. Just the two of us." Cal grinned. The past months had seen the Marine through tight spots. Cal trusted the sniper implicitly. Plus, he liked the idea of making Stricklin and Quailen a little uncomfortable.

"Where do you want us?" asked Gaucho.

"We'll wear earpieces. Listen up. We might have a nice conversation. You'll know if it's time to pounce."

+ + +

Minutes later, Cal and Daniel pulled up to the gate leading to Congressman Quailen's mansion. Cal pressed the button on the call box.

"May I help you?" came the scratchy voice from the box.

Cal waved to the camera, smiling. "Cal Stokes to see Congressman Quailen and Special Agent Steve Stricklin."

There was an extended pause, then the gate creaked open.

"So far so good," Cal murmured.

✦ ✦ ✦

"Looks like your old buddy's here," Quailen stated nonchalantly, walking into the library where Stricklin sat nursing another drink. He looked up with semi-bloodshot eyes.

"What? Who?"

"Stokes. He's coming up to the house right now."

"What?! How did he—."

"Settle down, Stevie. Looks like he's not as stupid as you let on. Let's just see how this plays out. He can't do anything with my security staff watching us."

Stricklin downed the rest of his drink and nodded, hoping his churning stomach wouldn't betray him.

✦ ✦ ✦

Congressman Quailen greeted the visitors at the door, two security personnel standing at the stairwell.

"Welcome, gentlemen. To what do I owe the pleasure?"

"Sorry to bother you at this hour, Congressman, but I received a phone call from this location, and since I was in the area, I thought I'd stop by and have a face-to-face," said Cal, casually.

"That's okay. You must be looking for my nephew."

Quailen chuckled at the confused look on Cal's face.

"Stevie, I mean Steve Stricklin, he's my nephew on my ex-wife's side."

"Right. He and I go way back."

Quailen nodded. "You're more than welcome to come in. I hope you don't mind if I have my bodyguards do a quick search?"

"No problem," said Cal, raising his hands good-naturedly. He wouldn't give the prick the satisfaction of being set back a single step.

+ + +

After a thorough frisking, no weapons were found, and neither were the tiny earbuds they'd implanted deep into their ear canals. They were led into the house.

"Would you like something to drink, gentlemen?" asked Quailen, playing the role of model host.

"I'll take some Jack if you've got it. On the rocks, please," requested Cal.

"And your friend?"

"He's fine."

Once Quailen had poured Cal a glass and topped off his own, they rounded a corner and entered the spacious library.

+ + +

"What do you mean he went in there?" asked Travis. "Is he fucking crazy?"

"Can't say I disagree with him," said Gaucho, who'd called Haden on Cal's orders.

"You wanna explain that to me, Gaucho? Don't you think it's a bit of a risk?" Travis fumed. Not only had his cousin repeatedly undertaken self-imposed assignments bordering on recklessness, now he was confronting a United States Representative *and* an FBI agent.

"We've got nothing right now. If Cal can get some answers, put the bad guys back on their heels, maybe something will open up. He's no idiot. Cal knows what he's doing."

Travis willed his temper under control. Maybe he was getting soft. It was something he'd talked to Todd Dunn about. Years of sitting behind a desk dulled the warrior within, whereas Cal continued to fight on the front lines. While the CEO in him doubted the tactics by which his Marine cousin exploited situations, most often being in your face, right up the middle, Cal got results. In the time since Cal had joined the ranks of SSI, operational effectiveness had increased dramatically. Cal's teams found and went after the bad guys, period.

"Okay. Let me know." Travis replaced the phone on his desk and ran a hand through his dirty blond hair. *What now?*

+++

"Stokes," sneered Stricklin, obviously drunk.

"Stevie, how the hell are ya?" answered Cal, raising his glass.

Quailen took the seat nearest the fire, enjoying the back and forth. "So how might we help you tonight, Mr. Stokes?"

"I got a call from your nephew about an hour ago. He wasn't very nice, so I thought I'd come over and see who pissed in your Wheaties."

"You know why I—."

"It's okay, Steve," interrupted Quailen. "I'm sure this is just a misunderstanding." He didn't want to make it easy for the upstart from Nashville. "How can we help you?"

Cal sipped his drink. There were several scenarios he could play. In the end he went with the most direct. "I'd like to know what evidence you think you have on me, Stricklin."

Stricklin looked at his uncle, who nodded. "We have documentation stating that your company was involved not only with the false allegation against my uncle, and the manufacturing of that ridiculous video, but also that you were key contributors in the attacks against the first lady in Washington, D.C. and Alabama."

Quailen waited. The part about their involvement with his video was true. His source had given him that piece of the puzzle. The other part, alleging SSI's involvement in the assassination of the vice president and the attempted murder of the first lady, had been fabricated by a very talented writer friend the congressman had used over the years to frame certain political opponents. Quailen had found early on that the truth almost never mattered. A simple allegation and a good story were usually enough to get politicians and their constituents in an uproar. The use of anonymous sources sprinkled with half-truths was one of the Louisiana congressman's favorite tactics.

"I don't know what you're talking about, Stricklin. You better get your facts straight before you come at me with some bullshit charge. Don't they teach investigative skills at the FBI Academy anymore?"

Before Stricklin could reply, there was a knock at the library door.

"I said we were not to be disturbed," yelled Quailen, looking annoyed.

"There's an important phone call for you, sir," came the muffled reply.

Quailen huffed and hauled his large frame out of the chair. "If you gentlemen will excuse me."

No one said a word as they waited. Cal took the opportunity to stand up and peruse the impressive collection of books arrayed neatly on the congressman's oak shelving.

Congressman Quailen re-entered, followed by members of his security detail. Cal looked up from his examination.

"Well, gentlemen, that was the president. He'd like us all to join him in the Oval Office."

"What's this about, Congressman?" asked Cal.

In response, Quailen shrugged, turning around, heading for the exit. Cal and Daniel looked at each other questioningly, and then followed Quailen and a slightly staggering Stricklin out the door.

Chapter 24
Falls Church, VA
12:22am, December 20th

"DID I HEAR that right? Did he say the president?" asked Gaucho. The other men in the SUV nodded. "I better call Travis."

✦ ✦ ✦

A driver pulled a black Lincoln Navigator up alongside Cal's vehicle. "We'll follow you?" suggested Quailen, standing on the other side of the vehicle, now wearing a heavy overcoat and a thick scarf that obscured half his face and muffled his voice in the cold air.

Cal nodded and went to open his car door. As he did, a loud *SPLAT* sounded, followed by a high-pitched scream.

Cal and Daniel crouched and moved around the black SUV. Stricklin stood screeching, illuminated by the bright porch light. Blood covered his face and front, as he looked down to where his uncle's body lay, head ripped in half like a dropped watermelon.

All of a sudden, security personnel swarmed the area, yelling for Cal and Daniel to get down on the ground.

"Whoa, whoa, whoa, guys. We're not armed," calmed Cal.

"Get down on the ground! Get down now!" came the repeated screams.

Cal looked at Daniel. Both men eased their way down to the ground as Cal whispered, "Gaucho, congressman down, unknown shooter."

✦ ✦ ✦

The helicopter banked to the south.

"Nice shot."

"Thanks. Easy."

The two men grinned as they settled in for the short flight back.

✦ ✦ ✦

"We didn't see where the shot came from. It could've been one of the guards with a silenced round for all we know," reported Gaucho.

"What are they doing with Cal and Daniel?" asked Travis.

Luckily, they'd kept all drones in the air during the wait, monitoring the situation on the ground. "It looks like they're loading them into one of the vehicles. Want us to bust in there?"

Travis didn't want a gun battle in the middle of the affluent neighborhood, but he didn't want his men captured either. "Follow them and we'll play it by ear. I'll wake the rest of the team and support you with whatever we can."

"You got it. All teams, time to duck and trail," Gaucho ordered, watching, waiting.

✦ ✦ ✦

"Where are you taking us?" Cal asked the driver. They'd been cuffed and latched to the child car seat tether anchored in the back of another Lincoln Navigator. The last he'd seen of the dead congressman was when they'd hauled his body away, along with his piss-stained nephew.

"Keep your mouth shut," said the burly man in the passenger's seat.

"Fine by me. Just wanted to make some pleasant conversation, fellas. You know we're not the bad guys, right?"

No response came from the driver or his companion. Cal could only hope that the cavalry wasn't far behind.

✛ ✛ ✛

"What happened?" Vice President Zimmer asked into the phone.

Travis told the former Senator everything he knew. "We've got a team following. Did you know anything about the president asking for a meeting?"

"I didn't," admitted Zimmer, wondering what else he wasn't being told.

"I think you better talk to him. I'll monitor the situation and keep you posted."

Zimmer was worried. The first lady's life threatened. A congressman murdered in the middle of a Virginia suburb. Cal and Daniel whisked away by a group of mercenaries. *What next?*

✛ ✛ ✛

Maynor was monitoring the situation from the SSI safe house. He felt helpless listening to radio chatter, wishing he could do something, anything to aid his fellow Marines. An idea came. He picked up his phone.

+ + +

"I didn't request a meeting. Who told you that?" asked the president, still wearing workout clothes from a late night basketball game with some of the White House staff.

Zimmer relayed what Travis had told him.

"Quailen is dead?" blurted the president.

"I'm afraid so, sir, and they've got Cal and Daniel."

"Who are *they*?" It wasn't good. The president had entrusted Stokes with the ability to take action. Just the thought of his asset falling into the wrong hands made his stomach turn.

"I have no idea, sir, I'm still new to the whole thing. Who would you like me to contact?"

"No one. Let's see if Cal can get out of this himself."

"But—."

The president raised his hand to stop the forthcoming rebuttal. "Look. If there's anything I've learned in the past year, it's that you should let good men do what they do best and leave them to it. The second we press the alarm button, half the politicians in this town, and not to mention the media, will know what's going on. I say we let SSI take care of their own."

Zimmer didn't like it, but he saw the president's point. It was what SSI did. Covert action. There was no one better group to rescue Cal than his own men. Zimmer exhaled. It was going to be another long night.

Chapter 25
Northern Virginia
1:10am, December 20th

CAL KEPT UP the charade and chatted like he was on a road trip with friends. He could tell that the driver was carefully covering his tracks, turning at the last second, zooming through a yellow light, backtracking.

"You guys are pretty good at this. You learn it overseas? Army?"

The guards continued to ignore his questions, instead glancing at the side mirrors.

"You have any water up there? I'm kinda thirsty." Knowing that his team was listening, Cal wanted to make sure they knew he was okay. The last thing he wanted was for them to make a foolish decision and do something reckless in the middle of a D.C. suburb.

+ + +

SSI's drones made the chase almost easy. Instead of having to stay within eyeshot, which would've been hard to do inconspicuously with the near empty streets, their vehicles maintained a loose web, never crossing paths with the vehicle being followed.

Guacho tapped his fingers on the dash. He knew Cal and Daniel could take care of themselves, and yet something felt wrong. It was like going on a raid knowing that you were probably walking into a trap.

It didn't matter. They wouldn't leave their men. Gaucho cracked his neck and focused on the picture streaming from his tiny drone.

+ + +

Maynor scribbled a note and left it on the kitchen table. Next, he downed the coffee sludge in the bottom of his mug, grabbed the keys to his rented Harley, and walked out into the chill. He had an appointment to keep.

+ + +

Their vehicle was just passing a hospital, but Cal couldn't make out the name from the distance. The driver pulled the wheel hard to the left. They went under a large hospital walkway, and then sped down a ramp. "Can you guys drop me off at the ER? My stomach's a little queasy from your shitty driving."

The man in the passenger seat whipped around, pistol drawn, aimed at Cal's face. "Time for you to shut your mouth, pretty boy. We're almost there."

+ + +

"Where did they go? Does anyone have eyes on?" asked Gaucho.

"Lost them when they went under that overpass," came the voice of one of the vehicles. "They didn't come out the other side."

"Me too. Anyone picking up audio?" said another SSI operator. They'd maintained radio silence, wanting to hear Cal, who was broadcasting on the same frequency through his earpiece. His voice had gone silent.

+ + +

Cal looked back to see a motorized gate slam down behind them. They were in an underground parking garage, except that there weren't any other cars. Worse still, Cal couldn't hear anything except a bit of static in his earpiece.

The Navigator eased it's way across the huge expanse, passing dimly lit pockets. No signs of life. Up ahead Cal saw a double door, light streaming from its seams.

"We headed to those doors?" asked Cal, hoping that the rest of the team could still hear him. No verbal answer came, but a smack from the butt of a pistol did. Cal's head snapped back to hit the leather seat behind him.

"I told you to shut up," sneered the man with the gun.

Cal glared at the man, hoping to have the chance to repay him soon.

✛ ✛ ✛

Gaucho directed his driver to pass by, casually. They saw the ramp underneath the walking bridge where they'd lost contact. He picked up his phone and dialed the only person he could think of who might be able to help. The call picked up on the first ring. "Yeah?" came the hoarse voice.

"Neil, we need your help."

✛ ✛ ✛

Four men, dressed identically to the escorts, also armed with submachine guns, emerged from the far door and helped unload Cal and Daniel. They were led through the double doors and into the brightly lit hallway. It smelled new. There were places along the wall that still had fresh drywall patches and had yet to be covered in paint.

Cal and Daniel exchanged looks. A second later, Cal felt a hand over his mouth and a familiar scent in his nostrils. He struggled, but couldn't stand up to the strength of the two thugs holding him or the power of the drug now entering his airway.

Cal and Daniel made the rest of the trip unconscious, each carried by a pair of mercenaries.

+ + +

"I've got the blueprints for the hospital. It looks like they just added a new wing," confirmed Neil.

"What about the parking garage? Is there another way in?"

Neil panned his view, maneuvering through the three dimensional schematic. "I've got multiple elevators and stair wells, but...hold on. It looks like there's a...yeah, there's a pathway that leads up to the main hospital and up to..."

"The helo pad," Gaucho finished with a groan, as he looked up at the sound of a helicopter thumping overhead. The aircraft rose and banked to the south. "Shit."

Chapter 26
Vienna, VA
1:56am, December 20th

"**WELL,** Mr. Maynor—."

"Please, call me Don."

The well-spoken crew-cut giant smiled. "I guess we got lucky on this one, Don. Perfect timing."

Maynor shrugged. "For me too. Like I said, came up here to visit some old buddies, but," he feigned an embarrassed look, "Lost a little too much money in a few card games. I won't even mention the chick I met at the bar. Need to make some money to get me back home. Luckily I called my buddy and he said you all might need some part time help hauling."

"And you said home is Florida?"

"Alabama. Orange Beach to be exact," corrected Maynor, sipping on the cup of coffee he'd been offered from the old pot percolating in the corner of the dingy trailer.

"Isn't that where the concert bombing was?"

Maynor nodded. "Sure was. Happened right before I left to come up here. Damn shame."

The big man nodded grimly. "Well, everything in your record checks out. No DUIs. No recent arrests. Your friend was right. We do need help. Just got a rush job. Big contract. You're lucky you called. We've got the other two contractors and had another coming at eight in the morning. You'd be taking his spot. How'd you know to call us so late?"

"Just gave it a try. Figured I could leave a message for the morning. Imagine my surprise when you picked up."

The big man chuckled. "Like I said, big contract. That means long hours for me." The man, who'd introduced himself as Gary, made some notes on Maynor's paperwork and stamped APPROVED in red at the top. "You ready to head over to take a urine test? Last step before we let you get a bit of rest and then you'll hit the road."

"Sounds good to me. Need to take a piss after all that coffee anyway." Maynor followed the hiring manager out the door.

+ + +

"What happened?" asked Neil, still scanning the hospital blueprints.

"A hundred bucks says they took Cal and Snake Eyes off in a helo. Neil, I need you to activate their beacons," said Gaucho.

Neil flinched. The thought of the homing beacons he'd invented and tested on himself still brought the phantom pain from where his ankle used to be. He now wore a prosthesis in its place, due to an old enemy severing his foot to get rid of the beacon implanted there.

After Neil's kidnapping, most of the operators and all the top leaders within SSI had agreed to have two such devices implanted. The reason for multiple beacons being twofold. First, the locator could only be used once for a three-hour period due to the high output signal emitted. After that, they would have to be extracted and replaced. Second, they'd learned a lesson with Neil's capture, and Todd Dunn, promising never to be without a backup again, suggested they implant two in different locations on each man. Redundancy. The locations of each beacon was a tightly held secret.

Neil pushed his chair over to another bank of computer screens and entered his access codes. Seconds later, Neil activated Cal and Daniel's beacons. He waited for the GPS locators to engage.

✛ ✛ ✛

"Here you go." Gary handed Maynor a plastic urine specimen cup. "Just bring it out when you're done."

"No pecker checker?"

"What was that?"

Maynor grinned. "Sorry. In the Corps we used to call the guys that watched us taking piss tests pecker checkers."

Gary laughed. "I like that. No. No pecker checkers here."

Maynor locked the bathroom door behind him, setting the cup on the sink. He checked his cell phone for calls or messages. Nothing.

Seeing no other options, he set himself to the task. A minute later, he emerged, sample in hand, only to be greeted by two nasty looking thugs pointing submachine guns at him.

"Did I miss something, fellas? Just taking a leak."

Gary walked back into the trailer. "Please come with us, Mr. Maynor."

The two men took up positions behind the Marine, one nudging him with the muzzle of his weapon. Maynor followed Gary into the cold, hands in the air, still holding the warm cup of piss.

✛ ✛ ✛

Neil followed the two tiny dots as they traveled across the screen. He'd alerted Travis, who was now on video along with Todd Dunn, Marge Haines and Dr. Higgins on one of the Neil's computer monitors.

"Where's he going Neil?" asked Travis.

"The helicopter keeps turning. He might be trying to avoid air space restrictions." Neil panned out, trying to make some sense of the helicopter's path. Much like the chase after the Navigator, the helicopter kept juking like it was trying to lose a tail.

"Is Gaucho following?" asked Dunn.

"As best he can. The aircraft's just too fast."

"What about the hospital? Did they leave anyone behind to take a look around?"

"Gaucho thought it would be better if they followed the beacons. Said it might cause too much of a commotion if they tried breaking into the parking garage. I think he's right," said Neil, still focused on the moving map in front of him.

All they could do now was watch and wait. The aircraft would have to land. Hopefully Gaucho's team could get there in time.

+ + +

Maynor was led into a third trailer. The smell of disinfectant hit him as they walked in the door. "Strap him down over there," ordered Gary.

"Does that mean I failed the piss test?" asked Maynor, not backing down, despite the amount of firepower aimed in his direction.

"Take off everything above his waist and strap him to the gurney. The others will be here soon."

The two thugs moved to do as instructed, but the scrappy Marine had other plans. With the cup of piss in hand, whose lid he'd loosened on the short walk over, he threw the contents in the face of the closest guard, who recoiled in disgust.

The second man hesitated long enough for Maynor to deliver a crushing boot to the man's knee. The guard crumpled, gun flying to the side as Maynor moved to meet the first man who was still wiping his face. Sliding into a kneel, the former Lance Corporal led with his fists, swinging time after time into the man's groin, finally felling the groaning enemy.

Maynor swung around, looking for Gary. He was waiting.

"Looks like it's just you and me, old man," said Gary. "I hope you don't mind, but I don't want to get my shirt dirty." The huge man carefully unbuttoned his dress shirt, revealing a chest, torso and arms covered in tattoos; tattoos that Maynor knew depicted white power.

+ + +

The helicopter touched down in a field next to the small mobile home complex in Fairfax, VA. Two bodies were unloaded and carried toward the trailer sitting a hundred yards from the impromptu landing zone. In under a minute the helicopter was back in the air, moving swiftly toward the Potomac.

+ + +

"You hear that? We're about to have company. I'd say you have about thirty seconds to get your licks in," laughed Gary, who loomed over Maynor like a mighty bear. The sound of a helicopter came and went. The machine guns were out of reach. The big man would get to him before he got his hands on a weapon.

Maynor smiled. "Okay, you big fucker. Show me what you've got." He stepped forward.

+ + +

The small caravan tore along the deserted roadway, following Neil's directions. "Come on, man, we gotta get there," murmured Gaucho, willing his team to close the gap.

Chapter 27
Fairfax, VA
2:20am

BREATHING HEAVILY, Maynor struggled to focus on his adversary. After delivering a single blow, the seemingly immovable giant had proceeded to methodically pound the old Marine.

"Had enough yet, old man?" said Gary, who was barely winded.

Maynor spat a gob of blood at the man's face. "Fuck you."

Another hammer strike crushed against the side of Maynor's head, and spun him to the ground. His world grayed as he barely remained conscious.

"What the fuck happened here?" came a shout from the door, followed by a blast of cold air.

"No problem, Doc. Just had to teach one of your patients a lesson."

Maynor tried to see who was talking, but couldn't through the blur.

"I told you they weren't to be harmed, and what happened to these two?"

"He's tougher than I thought. Sorry." The big man sounded contrite in the face of the newcomer's questioning.

"Strap him onto the gurney. They're bringing the other two in now."

Maynor felt himself being hefted into the air and then laid on something soft. His clothes were ripped off as he passed out.

+ + +

"Five minutes out," announced Gaucho, both to his team and to the staff listening in from SSI. "Any intel on the target, Neil?"

"I'm trying to patch into any overhead satellites, but none are available. I'll keep working on it."

Gaucho gritted his teeth, kicking himself for letting his friends be taken.

+ + +

"Make sure they're strapped down correctly. We don't want another incident like we had in Detroit."

"Yes, Doctor."

"Have the devices arrived?"

"I have them right here."

"Good. Get them prepped. I'll make the incisions once we've matched the codes."

"Yes, sir."

✛ ✛ ✛

Gaucho checked his weapon. He hated using suppressors. They always messed with the balance, and therefore proper aim, of a weapon. Regardless, the less attention they could attract the better.

"Two minutes," he announced, more for the benefit of those watching from headquarters.

✛ ✛ ✛

Cal's head swirled in the darkness. A smell assaulted his senses. *Am I in a hospital?* he thought groggily. He'd spent his fair share of time in hospitals over the years. The source of the smell came to him suddenly. *Betadine.*

Sounds came next. The clanking of metal and the murmur of voices. Cal tried to shake his head, but it hurt. He focused on the noise, pinpointing that it was coming from his left. He turned his head that way, slowly. Gradually, he opened his eyes the slightest bit, doing his best to see through the shimmery haze. As his vision adjusted, he observed a man in surgical scrubs, mask and blood-covered gloves bending over a prostrate form. From where he lay, Cal couldn't see above the patient's torso, but something felt familiar about the...

"Looks like one of our guests is awake," came the voice of the man who was now cutting into the person under the spotlight. "Please make sure he's properly restrained. Without anesthesia, I don't want him squirming when I make the incision."

+ + +

The SSI team parked blocks away from the trailer park, moving the rest of the way on foot. Fanning out with practiced precision, no one said a word as they followed Neil's guidance through their earpieces.

+ + +

"This one's done. Why don't you check the connection. I can sew him up after I finish that one," said the surgeon, pointing at Cal.

"Sure thing, doc."

Cal struggled against his restraints to no avail. He was still groggy from whatever sedative they'd given him.

"What are you doing?" Cal dared to ask.

The doctor turned his head to regard his next patient. "Just a little procedure. You look fit. You should come out of it even better than this one." He patted the thigh of his last victim and wheeled his chair over to Cal. "Now, this might be a little cold," the man said as he opened the prep kit and spread betadine on Cal's stomach.

"Get your fucking hands off of me."

"Or what?" The grizzly caricature looming over him chuckled, still wearing his gory gloves. He snagged a scalpel from the mayo stand and admired it in the overhead light. "This really is my favorite part. Now, if you'll be so kind as to—."

The trailer went pitch black, and then the shooting started.

+ + +

Gaucho and his boys had taken out three guards who'd been patrolling the exterior. Without a shred of discipline, or maybe it was a false sense of security, the men stood around a small fire, warming themselves when the death blows fell.

The twelve man team converged on the trailer registering Cal and Daniel's beacons. Seconds later, one man cut the power and the rest streamed in.

+ + +

Cal strained and pulled hard to the right, away from the entrance, finally toppling his gurney to the ground. He didn't have a clue who the gunfire was coming from, but the last thing he wanted was to get caught in the crossfire.

Screams and more gunfire. He heard moaning.

Finally the firing stopped. "Boss, you in here?" came a familiar voice.

"Over here," beckoned Cal.

Moments later, the lights came back on and Gaucho approached, weapon still at the ready. "You okay?"

"I'm fine. Just get me off of this thing."

Chapter 28
Fairfax, VA
2:46am, December 20th

THE SSI WARRIORS had done their job, killing everyone, including Gary the giant and the surgeon. They found Daniel and Maynor strapped to tables at the opposite end of the trailer. Both men stretched their sore extremities, Maynor accepting a ice pack from one of Gaucho's men.

"You waited long enough," observed Cal. "What happened?"

Gaucho told him the story of the chase and Neil's use of the implanted transponders. "I'm glad they put those things in you guys. Made me a believer, boss."

Cal nodded, taking in the room. Now that he could see, he processed the scene. The person being operated on next to him was the nearly decapitated and wholly unrecognizable body of Congressman Quailen. What had seemed so familiar was the scarf still draped around the cadaver's neck like a gruesome doll.

"Let's get these bodies out of here. Keep the congressman separate for now."

"Hey, Cal, I think you better come see this," said Daniel.

Cal walked over with Gaucho, Maynor already standing next to Daniel.

"What is it?"

Daniel pointed down at the blood-spattered table. "I think that's what they were going to put inside us."

Cal picked one of the black devices up. It was flat on one side, bulbous on the other with a thick stump the size of a man's pinky sticking out one end. The entire apparatus looked to be no more than five inches long and maybe three inches wide.

"Is this what I think it is?" asked Cal, shivering at the thought of having the instrument implanted in his body.

"That's an IED," said Daniel.

+ + +

"Zimmer."

"Brandon, it's Cal."

"Thank God. Are you okay?"

"A little shaken, but I'll be fine. Are you with the president?"

"He's in the other room. You want me to get him?"

"No. I think it's better if we come to you. We've got a stop to make, and we'll come by after that."

"Okay. I'll be waiting."

+ + +

"Has the doctor called?"

"Not yet. Want me to try him again?"

"Yes. We're about to miss our timeline."

+ + +

Three of Cal's team members had stayed behind to dispose of the bodies at the trailer park. Cal instructed the rest of them to take positions around the compound.

"On my mark. Three, two, one, go, go, go."

Daniel was the first over the fence, followed by the rest of the troops. The raid took less than five minutes, with none wounded on the SSI side. Ten minutes after arriving, the SSI squad departed.

+ + +

"What do you mean he's not answering?"

"He's not picking up. I called Gary too. Nothing."

"Get some men over there and figure out what the hell is going on!"

+ + +

The White House guards peered into the back of Cal's vehicle and took a step back. "The president's expecting us," said Cal.

The senior guard hesitated. "Sir, I..."

"Trust me." Cal winked. "Best if you forgot what you just saw."

The vice president had called earlier to tell them about the impending arrival of a Calvin Stokes. He hadn't said anything about the extra vehicles or the cargo.

The guard looked at Cal's identification card one last time, handed it back through the window, and waved the vehicles on.

+ + +

The president and the vice president looked up when the door to the situation room swung open and a person staggered in, slammed against the table, mouth covered with duct tape.

"Sorry to barge in like this, Mr. President," said Cal, followed closely by Daniel, Maynor and Gaucho.

"Who is...Congressman Quailen?" stuttered the president, rising to his feet.

"Yes, sir," Cal affirmed.

"But I thought you said he was killed," said an equally shocked Zimmer.

Cal pushed the bloody captive into one of the pristine leather conference chairs. "That's what we thought. Good 'ol Pete put on quite a show." Cal reached down and ripped the duct tape off the congressman's mouth. "Why don't you tell the president who *really* got shot."

Quailen stared at Cal, hatred burning. "I want my attorney."

"Wrong answer," said Cal, delivering a chop to the man's nose, instantly crushing the bridge, sending Quailen reeling, yelling curses.

"Is that really..."

"We're out of time, Mr. President. Either we get the information we need, or we let a bunch of crazy skinheads kill more Americans."

The president looked to Zimmer.

"Let's try this again. Who did you dupe into dressing up as you, only to be killed in your front yard?" asked Cal, hand poised to punish another retort.

Quailen wiped his broken nose gingerly with the back of his sleeve. "You people don't know a fucking thing. You think we live in a black and white world. Well, let me tell you something. We live in a world of gray. It's my world, not yours."

"Why don't you cut the crap and tell us who you had murdered," commanded the president, tired of Quailen's bullshit.

Congressman Peter Quailen looked up through bloodshot eyes and smiled. "Joel Erling."

✚ ✚ ✚

"Sir, I just got off the phone with our guys. They went by the trailer park and everything's on fire. The fire department arrived as they drove by."

"What?! What about the doctor?"

"I still haven't gotten him on the phone. I think we need to assume the worst."

"Push up our timeline. Our contact just phoned and said they've got Quailen."

"But, we only have two…"

"Just do it. If we can't get it done now, there may never be another chance."

Chapter 29
The White House
4:55am, December 20th

QUAILEN HADN'T said another word after telling the president about the death of the former Republican congressman from Colorado. In fact, instead of talking, Quailen started laughing like a madman, marveling at how easy it had been to dupe his weak-willed colleague.

Now secured by the Secret Service detail in a detention cell, the SSI contingent, along with the president and vice president, considered their options.

"This still doesn't explain his connection with the terrorists. Is it coincidence that Quailen and Erling, whom you recently outed, just happened to be part of the coordinated attacks against my wife? I find that very hard to believe." The president hadn't stopped pacing, even bumming a cigarette from the slightly awestruck Don Maynor.

"I don't know," replied Cal. "It's possible, but not likely. I'm more inclined to think that whoever was behind the attacks contacted Quailen, knowing he'd have nowhere else to turn. Dr. Higgins, our in-house interrogator, is on his way here. If anyone can get it out of Quailen, it's him."

"Cal, what about the phone call Quailen said he got from the president? Do you think he was bluffing?" asked Zimmer.

"Unless the president isn't telling us something, I do think Quailen's full of it. He seemed pretty sure of himself when we were at his place. Cocky son-of-a-bitch."

"He's been that way since I've known him," said the president, exhaling a plume of blue gray smoke. "Do you think my wife is really the target? Could it all be a ploy, when they're really after me?"

Cal shrugged. "Anything's possible, but those videos from Detroit seemed pretty convincing. She must've pissed off someone pretty bad. Is the first lady here?"

The president nodded. "She's in the residence. Had a helluva rough week. Even asked our physician for some pills to help her sleep. Last time I went up to check on her, she was fast asleep."

"What about protection? She's not planning any more events, is she?"

The president stopped pacing. "She has a brunch in a couple hours, but it's here. On top of that, they've doubled her protective detail."

Something still nagged at Cal, a detail they were missing. "Sir, are we any closer to finding out whether you have a leak in your administration, and if so, who that might be?"

"We're not. I've had the Secret Service re-check everyone that has daily access to me and my family. Nothing. Not even a whiff."

Cal didn't like it. He still felt like they were two steps behind while whoever was behind the attacks had free reign in their movements. "I suggest they try again. From what we gathered at the trailer park, my gut's telling me they're about to hit again."

+ + +

"You're sure everything's in place?"

"Yes, sir."

"Good. Tell him to proceed."

+ + +

Neil could feel himself getting close to the source. He'd built half a castle of energy drink cans just to stay awake. The rest of his team cycled in shifts, ensuring a steady churn of data. The computer genius was the only one who hadn't left the workspace. He'd monitored and guided the operators on the ground who'd conducted the rescue. Neil was the hub.

"Neil, I just got access to the phone records," came the voice from across the room. Neil looked up through his glasses.

"Which ones?" Neil felt like they were monitoring half of Washington, D.C.

"Congressman Quailen's."

"And?"

"He did receive a phone call from the White House last night."

"You're kidding."

"Nope. The call was made at 11:47. Want me to send you the link?"

"Already got it." Neil analyzed the record, but it didn't have the phone number of the caller, just the location. It would take more digging to find out the identity of the phone used to call Quailen's residence. *I better give Cal a heads-up.*

✛ ✛ ✛

"Thanks. Tell me when you find out." Cal stared at his phone, worried by Neil's revelation. He wasn't sure if he should even tell the president.

"Any news?" asked the president.

Cal hesitated. "It looks like there was a phone call made to Quailen's house, and it was from the White House."

"What? How is that possible?"

Cal didn't want to point any more fingers until he was sure. "Let me have another word with Quailen. Maybe he's had time to rethink his position."

+ + +

Cal and Daniel left the Situation Room, nodding to the agents standing silently outside the door. "Can you tell us how to get to where they're holding Quailen?"

The shorter Secret Service agent gave a quick rundown. "You want me to have someone take you?"

"I think I've got it. Thanks."

The Marines walked without talking, each lost in their thoughts. "I think this is it," Cal announced, pointing to a small door up ahead.

Daniel took the lead, knocking, then entering when no reply came from inside. The sniper stepped inside, Cal right behind, each scanning the observation area. No one was there. Both men unholstered their pistols and crouched low. Cal pointed to the interrogation room, which was shrouded in darkness with the lights off. Daniel nodded, moving forward.

A light switch perched next to the door leading into the detention area. Daniel flipped it. Cal peered into the brightly illuminated room. "Fuck."

Chapter 30
The White House
5:15am, December 20th

THE SECRET SERVICE agent knocked on the master bedroom door.

"Yes?" came the first lady's voice from within.

"Ma'am, you requested we escort you down to the dining room. Is now a good time?"

"Yes, please come in."

The agent looked around, extracted his service weapon, and stepped into the room.

+ + +

Cal's eyes widened. Inside the interrogation room, Congressman Quailen, hands cuffed to the table, lay back, head flopped over his chair, obviously dead. Even worse, lying in a pile next to the table were three Secret Service agents, blood pooling dark red on the travertine floor.

"Jesus," breathed Cal.

"Cal, the first lady," said Daniel, already on his way to the door.

Shaken from his momentary stupor, Cal ran after him.

✦✦✦

"I think I'll go up and see my wife. Might I suggest you gentlemen get some rest? I'm sure we can find you a spot if you need one," the president said as he stood and stretched. "As for me, I think I could use a quick shower and shave."

Zimmer, Maynor and Gaucho all rose and waited for the Commander in Chief to leave. "I think I'll do the same. You guys can head down to the locker room with me if you'd like," Zimmer offered, stifling a yawn.

Gaucho put a finger to his ear and blanched. His pistol whipped out a split second later as he bolted for the door. "The first lady!" he yelled to the stunned Secret Service agents as he ran through. Without a word, they took the lead, sprinting to the president's quarters.

✚ ✚ ✚

Luckily, Cal and Daniel had quite literally run into three Secret Service agents, still in PT gear, just coming off duty. The look in Cal's eyes and the drawn weapons said it all.

They reached the door leading into the first family's residence. Cal let the agents take the lead. With practiced precision, the president's protectors, who'd already alerted their cohorts, stacked up outside the entrance. The first man checked the door. Locked. "That's a reinforced door. I need to call down for the keys," he whispered.

"Can't you shoot it?" asked Cal, worried that the first lady might already be dead.

The agent shook his head.

✚ ✚ ✚

"Mr. President, we have to get you to safety," urged the detail commander.

"Goddammit, that's my wife and kids up there!"

"I know that, sir, but..."

"Let's go." They were only steps behind Gaucho's small band, who'd just passed them. The agent looked like he wanted to say something, but then remembered his own wife and kids.

"I'll lead the way, sir."

✚ ✚ ✚

By the time the keys got to the residence door, thirty agents waited, taut, ready to rush in.

"Go!" came the call. They swarmed in, all thoughts of their own safety deafened by the thought of a murdered first family on their watch.

They moved swiftly and methodically through the halls, sitting rooms and bedrooms. Screams told them they were getting closer. The troupe rushed forward, Cal and Daniel in their midst.

"Mommy!"

Turning a corner into the living area, Cal took in the scene. The president's daughters clung to each other in a far corner. They screamed again at the site of the agents rushing in, training their weapons on the man, one of their own, arm wrapped tightly around the first lady's throat, the other pressing a pistol to her ear.

"Jamison, put the weapon down!" ordered the first agent in the room. Cal and Daniel crept forward, affording themselves a better view.

"Fuck you! This bitch will die!"

"Then you'll die too. Put the—."

"I don't give a shit. At least I'll die happy knowing I took out *the whore*!"

The room went silent, except for the sniffling coming from the two girls.

"Put the weapon down, son." The president muscled his way forward, much to the objection of his defenders.

Agent Jamison laughed maniacally. "Maybe I'll make it a two for one, *sir*," he said with a sneer, still smart enough to cover his body almost completely with his captive and a love seat.

"Please, tell me what you want. I promise—."

"Promise! You know how much bullshit I've listened to in this place? This is the fucking White House! It was founded by great men. Great men who are rolling in their graves knowing a bitch whore sleeps in this house of honor. Lies! All lies! You people have no idea what it means to be American!"

The president put his arms up, stepping forward, shrugging off the hands of the closest agents. "Take me instead. Whatever you want, we can—."

Two shots went off, and the first lady went down.

Chapter 31
The White House
5:25am, December 20th

"**WHY?**" asked the president, cradling his wife, tears running freely.

"There's a time to talk and a time to shoot, Mr. President. This is what we do," answered Cal, who'd taken the second shot a split second after Daniel.

The first round had taken the first lady in the arm, but more importantly, hit Jamison enough to move him into Cal's shot, right in the face.

"I'm sorry we shot you, ma'am," apologized Daniel, who was kneeling to help.

The first lady smiled weakly, blood drained from her face. "I understand. Thank you for having the courage to do it." She lifted her good hand and stroked the side of her husband's face. "I'll be okay, honey. I've been through worse."

The president grabbed her hands and pressed them against his face. "I'm so sorry. We'll get these—."

"Sir, the doctor's here," said one of the agents.

The White House physician kneeled down next to the small crowd, doing a quick examination of the first lady's arm. "We won't know for sure until we take an x-ray, but it looks clean. Through and through. Let's get her down to the clinic and then to the hospital."

There was a rush of activity as the agents followed the doctor's instructions, loading the first lady onto a wheeled gurney. A minute later, the bandaged patient rolled toward the nearest elevator, the president walking alongside. The body of the deceased agent rolled out the opposite way.

"You've got some guts, kid," said Maynor, clapping Cal on the back.

"I didn't know you were up here."

"Saw the whole thing."

Cal grunted. "Can you still keep your mouth shut?"

Maynor laughed. "You think I'm stupid enough to piss *you* off?"

Chapter 32
SSI Safe House, Arlington, VA
12:17pm, December 20th

CAL DOZED on the couch, barely watching the news on the television. It was the tenth replay of the story coming out of the White House. According to the anchors, an unsuccessful attempt by a crazed former White House employee had been thwarted before anyone in the White House could be harmed.

It never ceased to amaze Cal how gullible the media could be. If it came from the White House, it must be true. He wondered what the Secret Service would tell Agent Jamison's family, or the families of the other deceased agents. His thoughts wandered to the men he'd lost over the years. He knew the depth of pain and second-guessing the president's detail was going through. There would be a full-scale investigation.

People would be allowed to hand in their resignations, all for the greater good. It was bullshit and Cal knew it.

That thought followed Cal as he drifted to sleep.

+ + +

"How are the kids?" the first lady asked.

"They're fine. The nanny has them. I told her to spoil them, give them anything they want," said the president, who hadn't left his wife's side except to see to the children.

"Have they found out what Jamison wanted? He was always so kind to the girls."

"They're looking into it. Lou said they should have something soon. Jamison was the missing piece. He wasn't alone."

The first lady blinked slowly, fighting the sleep that would soon claim her. "When you find out who it was, tell me. I want the world to know."

"I'm not sure if that's—."

The First Lady's eyes hardened. "Don't give me your line about secrecy. I was almost killed. Our children were traumatized. *You* were in danger. We need to stand and tell our enemies that we will not be put down."

The president nodded weakly. It wasn't an argument he was prepared to have at the moment. He'd save the discussion for later. She would see reason once she'd had time to think on it.

Chapter 33
United State Naval Observatory
U.S. Vice President's Residence
6:20pm, December 20th

VICE PRESIDENT ZIMMER had invited the entire SSI team to his new home. He wasn't married, and he didn't want to eat alone. Too many things had happened in the past week to be by himself. For the third time that night, he shook his head thinking about the company he now kept. Before meeting Cal, he never would have imagined having friends like these. He'd changed. He'd changed a lot.

"I've got a club soda and a whiskey. Whose is whose?" he asked walking back into the spacious living area. Two of the operators raised their hands, and Zimmer delivered their drinks.

"You know you don't have to do that, right? We're big boys," said Cal, sipping on his own hefty pour.

"Let's just say that we owe you guys. Besides, I've got staff wiping my ass after I go to the bathroom now. I need to stay humble somehow."

Cal shrugged. "Your choice, but if you keep serving Gaucho like that he's liable to think you're part of *his* staff now."

Gaucho flipped Cal the finger and grabbed his crotch. "This is the only staff I need, jarhead."

Zimmer laughed along with the men, all of whom came from a very different world than the new vice president. A tinkling bell sounded from some unseen source.

"That means dinner's ready," Zimmer said, rolling his eyes at the throwback to royal service.

The warriors didn't need to be told twice. Drinks in hand, they followed the vice president to the dining room.

✛ ✛ ✛

"Sir, we've tracked down two of Jamison's accomplices. Looks like they were going to make another try at the first lady's brunch this morning," informed the Secret Service agent.

"Do you have them in custody yet?"

"We have teams deployed, sir. Should be in our hands soon."

"Any word on who they are?"

"Yes, sir. We believe the mastermind is a gentlemen named Evans Carlisle. He's suspected to be the head of a white brotherhood network, sort of a connector. The other suspect is his right hand. We don't have all his information yet."

"Motive?"

The agent looked uncomfortable. "Our guys think it's in line with what Jamison said to you."

"So it's all because of race?"

The agent shrugged.

"Okay. Thanks, Lou. Tell me when you have the suspects in custody."

"Yes, sir."

The president sat back in his chair and sighed, wondering if the issue of race would ever be resolved. He'd changed. His views had shifted along with his focus as president. Why couldn't others do the same?

+ + +

Two Secret Service Emergency Response Teams (ERTs) descended on the wooded complex nestled in the modest Vienna, VA suburb. Multiple K9 units accompanied the raid, as well as members of the Counter Sniper Unit. They weren't taking any chances. Local law enforcement was not informed.

Minutes after entering the two-story residence, agents positively identified the bodies of Evans Carlisle and Nicholas Rindle. The bodies were tested and death had been estimated six to eight hours earlier. In addition to the bodies, files and maps were discovered detailing the entire scheme, along with additional event details gleaned from the first lady's schedule, allegedly supplied by Special Agent Jamison.

Chapter 34
The White House
8:40am, December 21st

"**THANKS FOR** stopping by, Cal. I know you've got a flight this morning."

"Not a problem, Mr. President. I've got time. How's the family?"

"They're coping."

"And the first lady?"

"She's tough. A few scrapes won't keep her down. Hell, sometimes I think she's tougher that me."

"It sounds like the Secret Service has things wrapped up," said Cal, preferring to talk business.

"Looks like it. They think this Carlisle guy," the president waved a folder, "and his pal took their own lives when they knew they couldn't get away. Same thing happened up in Minnesota. Tracked the guys down only to find him with a gun in his mouth. He pulled the trigger just as the police busted in."

"That's too bad. I hope you get the whole story before this is over."

The president nodded. He looked tired. Not tired — weary. Weary of the weight on his shoulders. Cal swore the man looked grayer than he had a day before.

"Anything I can do for you before we leave, sir?" Cal asked, shaking the president from his thoughts.

"You've done more than I could've asked. Please thank your men for me. Maybe I'll stop by the next time I'm in Nashville."

Cal couldn't believe himself, and yet he said, "I think they'd like that, sir."

"And you?" the president asked, a slight grin tugging at the corner of his mouth.

"I don't know. Maybe I'm getting used to you politicians."

Both men shared a laugh, each considering the unlikely alliance between stubborn Marine and a Democrat president.

"Well, I should be going."

"Yes, do you need a ride?"

"I'll take a cab, sir. More inconspicuous."

They said their goodbyes and the president led Cal to the gate, agents flowing around silently. Cal slipped into the taxi cab and waved as they headed to Reagan International.

+ + +

"Hey, I'm on my way to the airport."

"Cal." Neil, hesitated, something he never did.

"What is it?"

"I found out where the calls were coming from. It wasn't Jamison."

"Tell me."

+ + +

The president took a hitched breath and opened the master bedroom door. Cal and Dr. Higgins followed.

The first lady, wearing a pearl silk nightgown, arm strapped in a sling, sat at her vanity, applying makeup. She scowled slightly when she noticed the extra guests.

"Is everything okay, honey?" she asked sweetly, suddenly unperturbed by the company. Awkwardly, she continued with her eyeliner.

"Why did you do it?" asked the president, quietly.

"Do what?"

The president shook his head. "All those people. Our children. You put them in danger."

The first lady slowly put her eyeliner pencil on the table and turned to face her husband. She rose to her feet, scowling.

"What do you think you know?"

"We know it was you behind the attacks. Why? Why would you do something like this?" the president's words came out haltingly.

Her face morphed, angry, sinister. "Who told you? Was it him? Was it Cal the fucking Marine? You'd believe him over me?"

The president's head snapped up at the hate in his wife's voice. "That's enough. We have all the proof we need. Cut the show and tell me why."

The first lady smiled smugly. "You think you're the smart one in this family? You think you know how to run a country? Ha! You'd be nothing without me! Do you know how many things I did to get you in office, to keep you in office?"

The president's face paled.

"Oh, don't looked so shocked, *honey*. While you were off on your hope and change kick, looking good for the cameras, I was in the background, doing the deals you've always said you were too good for. You have no fucking idea!"

Shaking his head, trying to understand the stranger standing in front of him, the president asked, "How did you do it? Why would a man like Carlisle—."

"Why would he do it? Are you kidding? He's the worst kind of racist. All I had to do was some digging and find out who hated me the most. There are whole websites dedicated to seeing my head cut off, so I used it. I used my enemy as my ally. He never knew I was behind it, and neither did Jamison. I bet you didn't know about his past, did you?"

"How did you?"

"Let's just say I used my assets. Even a racist can't say no to the president's wife," she said lasciviously.

"I...I don't know you anymore." The president looked like he was about to fall over. Cal gave an arm to steady him. The president took it, his head hanging.

"Oh, please. I did this for us, for you. Do you know where our poll numbers will go when news of white supremacists trying to kill the black first lady gets out? They'll change the Constitution, give you a third term, in a landslide!"

The president's head rose slowly. He looked back at Cal, the pain causing his eyes to look like marbles in a deep pit. "We'll take care of it, sir. You don't need to be here," said Cal, truly sad for the president.

The leader of the free world, now brought to his knees, nodded and stumbled to the door.

"What are you going to do, kill me?"

"No, ma'am." Cal closed the gap as the first lady raised her good arm protectively. The Marine grabbed her wrist, forcing the arm down, using his other hand to get a grip on the first lady's neck. "Doc."

Dr. Higgins, portly and normally congenial, extracted a syringe from his tweed coat pocket, taking off the safety cap. "Hold her still, Calvin."

The first lady's eyes bulged. "What are you doing?! NO! NO!"

In the hallway, the president went to his knees, sobbing uncontrollably.

Chapter 35
Camp Spartan, Arrington, TN
10:29am, December 22nd

CAL INVITED Don Maynor to visit SSI, promising to show him around Nashville as thanks for helping with the recent operation. Maynor didn't need much coercion. He readily agreed and had flown to Nashville with the rest of the team.

They all sat in the lodge's spacious lounge, enjoying a much-needed drink, swapping stories, waiting for the news conference. Cal hadn't planned on watching, having already put their latest excursion behind him. It had been incredible, but to the battle-hardened warrior, it was just another operation.

The only reason he'd decided to have the president's address on was because the president had called early that morning, requesting Cal to tune in.

"I can't do much in the way of a public thanks, but I'll do what I can," the president had said.

So Cal had gathered up the crew who'd been in D.C., along with Travis, MSgt Trent, Marge Haines, Todd Dunn and Dr. Higgins. Cal chuckled at the endless back-and-forth between the near seven foot Trent and the five-foot-nothing Gaucho. Half the room was in stitches at their ribbing.

"Here he is," someone announced, as the president appeared on the large television screen, stepping up to the podium. To Cal's trained eye, the man looked older. How could you blame him? He'd lost his wife twice in one day. Behind him, Vice President Zimmer stood stoically.

"Ladies and gentlemen, thank you for coming at such short notice. Before I start, I would like to say that I will not be taking questions today." There were murmurs from the gallery. The media honeymoon had come and gone since the president's first term, replaced by prearranged questions and less access for reporters. "I have prepared a few words that I hope will shed light on recent events. First, I would like to thank the members of local law enforcement and our federal agents who assisted in the investigations into the attacks here in the capitol and in Alabama. Also, I send my thoughts and prayers, along with the rest of America, to those who lost loved ones. We are with you and will not rest until each and every criminal is brought to justice for these heinous acts. There are also some unsung heroes, who I wish I could mention by name, but who played a pivotal role in bringing closure to the investigation. I know you're watching, and I say, from the bottom of my heart, you are heroes, and will always hold a special place in my heart."

The president paused, looking down from the camera. His shoulders seemed to sag a bit as he continued. "A few of you know by now that last night, my wife, the first lady, suffered a severe stroke. I am being told by the best doctors that she will not regain normal function. She is, essentially, alive, but in a vegetative state."

This was news to the assemblage, as evidenced by questions being shouted at the podium. The only information previously released from the White House had been that the first lady was taken in for some kind of minor seizure, reportedly something she'd had since childhood. This was a revelation. It was shocking. More than one intrepid reporter found tears in their eyes.

The president raised a weary hand for silence.

"As you can imagine, the loss of a loved one is debilitating. It hurts you to your core. I...I don't know what I'll do without my beautiful wife...my girls...my..."

The hushed silence was punctuated by the repeated clicks from photographers, the whir of the small fans lining the stuffy room.

With a handkerchief pulled from his pocket, the president wiped his eyes. "I'm sorry. As you can imagine, it's been a rough night." No one said a word. Everyone waited for more. Would there be more? The president coughed into his hand, squared his shoulders, and looked directly into the camera. "Due to my wife's condition, its effect on my daughters, and myself...effective immediately, I resign my position as President of the United States." Gasps from the crowd. "Also effective immediately, the next President of the United States, a man I trust and admire, is Brandon Zimmer."

Every camera in the room zoomed in on the shocked face of now-President Brandon Zimmer, who mutely shook his predecessor's hand until the former president walked behind the curtain.

Cal stared up at the television. "Holy crap."

+ + + + +

Thanks for reading *PRESIDENTIAL SHIFT*. If you liked the book, please take a minute and write a review. Every review helps the success of this book.

Also, please consider sharing this book with your friends via email and social media.

To hear about new books first, **and to get any *Corps Justice* novel for FREE**, sign up to my New Release Mailing List at www.CorpsJustice.com.

Follow us on Facebook at
http://www.facebook.com/CorpsJustice

Questions For The Author?
Email me at Carlos@CorpsJustice.com

SEMPER FIDELIS